Life of a Firefly

THE INCREDIBLE ADVENTURES AND MOSTLY TRUE STORIES OF SANDY FORTE

SANDRA BROWN LINDSTEDT

Illustrated by SUZANNE GROAT

Adapted from
I Am Fireflies Ascending © Sandra Brown Lindstedt 2015
ISBN 978-91-88023-23-0

This book is a personal account based on childhood memories, which have
been slightly altered for dramatic purposes. Any people or persons, either
real or imagined are merely a composition of characters and not to be
taken as a factual representation of anyone.

Life of a Firefly © Sandra Brown Lindstedt 2020
Follow the author: sandylinnbooks.com
sandy@sandylinnbooks.com
Cover illustration: Marlon Hall
Illustrations: Suzanne Groat
Cover design and interior layout: Keith Tarrier

First edition
ISBN 979-8-6791-3332-7

PRAISE FOR
Life of a Firefly

- Winner 2021 INTERNATIONAL BOOK AWARDS, Children's Mind/Soul/Body
- Winner Reader Views' 2020-2021 GRAND PRIZE

I really enjoyed this story! I have a seven-year-old daughter who absolutely loved to read this! I love how quick witted and courageous Sandy is, and the way you weave the lessons she learns in church and from her family into each story is beautiful! Several times, I found myself laughing at her antics and responses.

Sandy takes us through a journey of her life, from childhood through her early teen years. It is filled with faith and wonder! Each person she encounters teaches her a lesson about life, God, faith, and herself. This was a beautiful tale that will remind children that no matter how bleak a situation may look, a little faith, or a firefly, can take them a long way. This book needs to be in every elementary and middle school library in the US! Not only does it give black children a chance to read books with strong characters who look like them, it also helps to humanize the black community to those outside of it. Well done!

—Megan B. Joseph: MHA

I can't even express how much I LOVED this book. Usually in a full calendar year I come across one or two books (if I'm lucky) that really stand out. Yours is one of those books. In fact, it's one of the best books I've read in the past decade. If you think about all the books that are published and sitting on shelves, and the small percentage that actually do make it to a best-seller list, maybe this will put things into perspective in what I'm trying to say about how special your book is. I really, truly mean that this book is exceptional, and it can stand out among all of its competitors. You have a gift of storytelling, and it's a magical thing to read and experience! I loved every moment of this story, and Sandy is the perfect protagonist. I have no doubt that your readers will love this story!

—Ms. Allison, Editor with Book Editing Services

"There are so many great adventures in this book and Sandy's journey is one that will stay with the reader for a long time after they finish reading. The writing is amazing, the characters are genuine and the author paints pictures with her words. I highly recommend this book to teens and older.

—Amy C (age 16) for Reader Views Kids (02/2021)

Acknowledgements

A special thanks to all the children of the
International School of Gothenburg, Sweden.
Thank you for inspiring me to write this book.
And to my husband, Christer, whose
encouragement and painstaking perseverance
made this book what it is today.

CHAPTERY

CHAPTER 1

MISS BECKY AND THE SILENT SISTER

Hey Sister girl, now what you got to say?
Don't sit there, head down, like you fend to pray
Sister girl, you hear me?
I said what's wrong with you?
Black cat got yo' tongue and his white devil too?
Baby girl, open yo' mouth
and use dem pretty words
I'll give you chiffon pie, with sweet lemon curd
All right dat's it. Now I gits my switch
God knows I ain't trying to raise no lil' witch!

The sky was black as blood pudding, but our front yard was filled with swarming lights. The entire town smelled of honeysuckle and fresh-cut jasmine. My bare feet raced through the wildflowers that grew around the tall maple tree. It was planted by my great-uncle Lloyd. I ran faster, grabbing at the jasmine-scented air until I caught hold of a light. I held it tightly in my hand, waving my fist above my head.

"I dare you!" Glory said.

"What you gonna give me if I do?" I asked.

1

"Uhhh, my new pencil," she answered.

"I want the silver crayon from the *new* box."

"Red."

"Silver!"

"Well . . . okay," she said reluctantly.

Then I swallowed the firefly.

I just popped it in my mouth, took a deep breath, and swallowed hard. I didn't expect it to go down so easily, but it did. Then Glory pulled up my t-shirt to take a look at my belly just as Grandma came out on the porch swinging her large wooden spoon.

"Sandy! Glory! Y'all might be as black as coal dust, but I see y'all rippin' and runnin' through my flowerbeds. Now git!" she yelled. We both ran screaming and hid behind the big maple tree.

"Young Philistines," she mumbled, as she went back into the house.

Glory was always daring me to do this or that, like touch electric wires or climb into hog pens or jump off the smokehouse roof. I always did it because she was my big sister, and with age comes authority.

Now she resumed the inspection of my belly. "Awww . . . ain't nothin' happen." Disappointed, she went into the house letting the screen door slam behind her.

I patted and rubbed my stomach, hoping to move the little insect into motion and to urge its light to come on. Nothing. The screen door opened and Glory stomped over with the silver crayon in her hand. It was from the box that held her prized collection. Looking down at the red dirt, she slowly handed it to me, and without any hesitation, I grabbed it and ran inside.

I found my coloring book under my bed in the corner. Now I could finally finish the unicorn's tail and horn. Glory came in and plopped down next to me. I thought she just wanted to make sure I didn't go outside the lines, but then she got up and left without saying a word.

✳ ✳ ✳

I arrived on the Earth, February 2, 1954 at a charity hospital in Chicago on one of the coldest days of the year. Actually, I was born in the elevator on the way up to the delivery room. It happened so fast, my mama didn't even have time to be amazed. I grew up partly in Texas, partly in Illinois. I guess my mama couldn't make up her mind. My mother named me Sandy because of the sandy color of my hair. To me it seemed a strange reason to name a person. What if my hair had been black or red or yellow? Now there weren't many enchantments or miracles back then, only a series of happenings, mistakes, and muddy memories as I'd like to call them.

My first muddy memory and the beginning of my mistakes started in 1957. I was three-years-old and Glory was five. We lived in a tiny red house in Hooks, Texas, with Uncle Timmy who was fifteen, and my grandmother, Miss Minnie Bell Forte. Grandma was around sixty years old—I'm guessing because who could really know how old their grandma was. I hold onto this memory because it was the summer that two important things happened:

my mother, Janetta Mae, left us and went back to Chicago and, on the very same day, I almost got my right foot cut clean off.

Janetta Mae hadn't been gone no more than a few hours when it happened. I was out running free and wild in the tall grass on the far side of Grandma's house. My uncle Timmy was mowing the lawn, and I guess he didn't see me when I fell, because the next thing I remembered there were a lot of tall men yelling and running as Uncle Timmy picked me up and carried me inside the house. The tall men were Uncle Timmy's friends who'd just happened to come by so they could all go fishing. Grandma poured warm coal oil from our lamp all over my foot. I screamed so loud that heaven shut her windows. I thought she was trying to burn me alive, but she was only encouraging my foot to heal. Uncle Timmy would nearly faint at any sight of blood, so he held me down with his eyes closed. Grandma wrapped my foot in a clean white dish towel to stop the bleeding. I suppose I should have gone to a hospital, but we lived too far away from town and besides, nobody owned a car.

I cried loudly for my mother that night, only to be reminded that she was probably arriving at the Union Station in Chicago by then.

After my mother had gone, everything seemed to change, even Glory. At night, we used to make up silly knock-knock jokes, but then the silence took over. It was like Glory was still there—but not. There were a lot of serious, quiet gazes. I would see her and even touch her, but I could hardly ever hear her, because she rarely spoke. Instead of telling me her secrets, she chose to write them in her diary. This went on for many years, prompting Grandma to call her the silent sister.

My next memory was two years later when my Aunt Sarah returned home from college for winter break. I thought she was the most beautiful creature I'd ever seen. Her smooth, ebony skin glowed in the flickering lamplight. She had black curly hair and wore dark red lipstick that made her teeth look like a string of white pearls. Sometimes she would sit cross-

4

legged on the floor in her wide pink poodle skirt and read to Glory and me exciting stories about pirates, slaves, and kings from her literature books. When it was story time, we'd follow and watch her open her big suitcase to see which book she would choose.

"Today is Christmas Eve and I've decided to read to you all a story from the Bible," she said.

"Awwww, nooo!" we said in unison.

"It's about the birth of Jesus. And it's not a fable like the others, but it's about a true Christmas miracle."

"Noooo!" we cried again. Aunt Sarah grabbed our hands and pulled us down to the floor facing her.

"*And* it's about this mean, old king named Herod, who was outsmarted by three wise Black kings from Africa. These kings were so rich that they brought bags of gold, incense, and myrrh just for Jesus' baby shower."

"What's incense and myrrh?" I asked.

"Well now, just you be quiet and listen like Glory and um gonna explain."

I watched her red lips move as her raven-like black eyes darted over the pages. I hoped that one day I would grow up to be just like her, a free form of melted molasses pouring out fountains of knowledge into eager clay pots.

Later that day, Grandma came back from what she called the *rag pile*, about a mile from our house. That was where she would go looking for odds and ends that the White people in our town would throw away as rubbish. She'd brush the snow from her wool winter coat. And after she'd taken off her muddy boots, she'd plop down by the black coal-pipe stove in the living room. We all gathered around as she opened her big orange and yellow-flowered bag. The wider she pulled open the strings, the bigger our eyes grew.

"If you gits there early enough, you kin find a lotta nice things,"

Grandma would say with a smile in her voice. And so she did. She'd found bits of yarn and pieces of gingham cloth that she'd use to make our Christmas presents. She also managed to find small, copper pots and pans for baking. She would scrub the copper pots until they shone like new pennies. As she baked, the smell of her chocolate teacakes and pecan pies filled the kitchen. It made my stomach growl like a baby polar bear. I wanted to sample everything, but Grandma would make us eat supper first.

That night Glory and I watched as scraps of thread and pieces of cloth turned into pretty, little dresses and dolls with smiling faces. *Could this be another Christmas miracle?* I wondered. Grandma's hands pulled the fabric effortlessly across her old Singer sewing machine as her foot peddled the lever in perfect harmony. She gathered cotton from an old pillow and stuffed it into worn socks, making the body of two rag dolls. Then, she sewed on glass buttons for eyes, red felt for lips, and black yarn for their hair that she tied in two ponytails with white ribbons. When she was finally done, the dolls looked like something you'd see in the window of Goldman's department store or in a Sears catalog.

When Grandma gave me my doll, I snatched her up and ran to my hiding place behind the big dresser. I'd never had anything that belonged just to me. I always had to share everything with Glory, even the prize from the Cracker Jack box. Once, she told Grandma there wasn't a prize in the box, even though I knew the people in the factory would never forget to put one in. Later, Uncle Timmy found the prize hidden behind the wood box in the kitchen. It was a whistle that he kept for himself.

As I looked into the kindness of my new friend's eyes, I could only think of one name for my doll: *Rebekah Jane Savannah Forte.* I found Glory sitting by the Christmas tree staring at her doll.

"What you gonna name yours?" I asked.

"Only real people got real names. Umma jus' call her Doll."

Well, I didn't agree with that at all. But I'd never say that to Glory.

6

She was, of course, my big sister. And back then, I thought big sisters were never to be told they were wrong about anything. Before I went to bed, I decided to ask Grandma.

"Glory said only real people got real names. Cain't I name my doll if I want to?"

"What did you name her?" she asked, as she pulled the quilt over me.

"Miss Rebekah Jane Savannah Forte. But I just calls her Miss Becky."

"Well now, that's a real powerful name. How'd you come up with it?"

"The first part was from a story that Aunt Sarah told us. It was about a girl who saved her whole family from mean slave traders in Mississippi. And the last name of course is mine."

"Well, my Bible says a good name is rather to be chosen than great riches, and loving favor rather than silver and gold. So now, say your prayers and go to sleep."

That night, I thought long and hard about what Grandma had said. I didn't know what any of it meant at the time, but it made my feelings quiet down until there was only the sound of Grandma's humming coming from the kitchen.

We carried our dolls everywhere we went. Grown-ups would stop us on the street and ask me about Miss Becky. White people as well as Black wanted to know where to buy them.

When it was time for Aunt Sarah to go back to college, we all went to the railway station in downtown Texarkana to give her a proper goodbye. That's when a White lady stopped us on the street, right in front of Betty Joe's bar and grill.

"Where did you get these pretty little dolls? I'd love to buy one for my daughter. Are they handmade?"

"No," I said. "Dey made by my grandma. Dey made from rags she got outta the rag pile."

"Hush up, Sandy," Uncle Timmy said, pulling me to one side. "Don't tell folks dey comes from the rag pile. Say yo' grandma bought it for you."

"But dat ain't true! Dey is come from the rag pile," I said louder this time.

"Mind yo' big sister and do like she do. You see Glory knows when to be quiet," Uncle Timmy whispered so people wandering out of the restaurant couldn't hear.

That was true. Going from totally silent to selective, Glory seemed to have a little policeman with a whistle inside her head that let her know when to say what. I didn't have anybody in my head telling me when to shut up. Most of the time words came out of my mouth so fast that I would stutter, trying to get them all to make sense. But it was right then that I realized there must be something terribly wrong with getting things from the rag pile and it was much better to buy new things from the store. So I kept my big mouth shut.

$$* \quad * \quad *$$

"Sandy! Glory! Git cleaned up and make sure you use plenty of Ivory soap. Supper's ready!" Grandma yelled from the kitchen.

After chasing our rooster back from Miss Lettie's house across the road, I started to feel the hunger pangs banging like a drum inside my stomach. I skipped washing up and ran inside. Glory came in later, her hands still wet from washing and sat down at the table.

"Sandy didn't wash," Glory said.

"Did so," I lied.

"Hold out yo' hands and let's see," Grandma said.

"Awww, alright, alright. But why you need clean hands just to eat supper?" I whined as I got up and went on the back porch, grabbed the soap, and washed my hands in the wooden bucket by the door.

Grandma never complained too much about anything, not even my constant talking. As a matter of fact, she seemed to enjoy it. Like when she would read to us from her big, white Bible every night by the amber glow from the oil lamp. The flicker of light would make her brown cinnamon-colored skin glow. Her high cheekbones and swirls of silver-streaked hair spoke of her African and Native American ancestors. After reading a scripture, she would try to explain to us what it all meant.

"Suffer the little children to come unto me, and forbid them not, says the Lord."

"But, why do the children have to suffer? Is Jesus real mean?" I asked.

"Well now, to suffer right heah means to *allow*. Jesus ain't never been mean." Then she'd point to a picture in her Bible of Jesus surrounded by smiling children.

"Then why don't he jus' say allow and leave the sufferin' part out?" I said. Grandma would just smile at me and pat me on the head. As I'd turn the thin, delicate pages, I was sure I would be able to find even more errors in her big Bible, if time permitted.

"So . . . what y'all wanna talk about today?" Grandma asked as she settled into her big chair.

I loved when she asked that question because she seemed to be filled with lots of wonderful stories, some scary, some funny, but always interesting. Sometimes she'd tell us stories about her life and little snatches of our family tree would come out.

"When you was little!" I yelled.

"Now let's see. Yo' great-grandmother, my mother, was a full Blackfoot Indian. My daddy—Lucius Brown was his name—was a real Black cowboy from Louisiana. Now, his mama and daddy was slaves out thare in Jackson County. But after the war, when theys all freed, they left Louisiana for Montana. Daddy was a ranch hand, skilled at taming young, wild horses. And back then, Mama was a young girl livin' on a reservation. One day, Daddy took a notion and rode out to where she lived. Well suh, Daddy took one look at Mama and he was smitten. The next day, he comes a-ridin' in on his big horse and jus' swoops Mama up and keeps on ridin'. Didn't stop 'til he gits clear out to the state of Texas and on into Red River County."

"But Grandma, ain't that like kidnapping somebody?" I asked.

"Oh no, child. Ain't like dat at all. No suh. It was the Lord's will I 'spect, 'cause they grew to love one another."

I got closer, looking deep into my grandmother's eyes. "But how you know it was the Lord's will? Did he send you some kind of message?"

"Well now you see, it's like this heah. I knows for sho' it was God, because if he hadn't done it, I wouldn't be heah. Neither would all of my nine sisters and brothers—your mother and you and Glory wouldn't be heah either. A whole generation of folks was just waitin' on Daddy and his horse to come a-ridin' in that day lookin' for Mama. Anyhow, now that you got me thinking back, it may have started out as an unholy act, but God knows how to turn things 'round. And befo' Daddy died, he went back to Montana to that reservation and made it right with the big chief. Daddy won over his heart so much dat the chief gave Daddy dis heah leather chain as a peace offerin'."

She carefully unfolded a handkerchief she kept in her apron pocket, revealing a colorful, red-and-yellow armband made of rawhide. Glory and me both tried to grab the band to be the first to put it on.

Now, I wasn't sure how much of this story was true and how much was fable. But that night, with Miss Becky beside me, I lay awake for hours, imagining what it would be like to be a young Blackfoot Indian squaw living in a teepee on the reservation. I'd picture myself out in a field gathering ripe corn in my apron,or weaving baskets from dried husks and painting them with dye made from the earth and red flowers. I imagined that if I needed a new coat, I'd stretch deer hide and hang it out to dry in the sun. As I fell asleep, I could almost smell the aroma of salmon smoking over coals in the fire pit.

CHAPTER 2

AND IN THAT HOLE

Time and seasons passed almost unnoticed until there was an interruption. Almost like looking up and seeing a star suddenly fall from the sky without any warning. It was late October 1960, and I was almost seven years old. After three years of living in the tiny town of Hooks, Uncle Timmy was fixing to take Glory and me back to live with our real mother, Janetta Mae, in the big city of Chicago. Janetta Mae had written a long letter to Grandma saying how she wanted Glory and me to go to school in the city. She said she had gotten a new job in a factory called Dixie Cup making paper cups, paper plates, and such things. She said she even got to wear a white uniform just like a nurse.

As Grandma read the letter to us, I tried to imagine what it would be like to not hear her voice calling to me every morning. But then my imagination turned to happier thoughts. Eventually it began to catch fire! It started to grow hotter and hotter until I was overflowing with excitement. I would finally get to see my mother in real life and not just a water stained picture on Grandma's dresser. I really couldn't make out her face very well, but I never forgot what her voice sounded like. It wasn't like Grandma's at all. It was deep and low, like a windstorm whispering through loose boards in our ceiling.

I wondered if my mother would remember what we looked like,

because me and Glory had changed so much. In the years since she'd gone, I'd lost two teeth. Grandma had taken a long piece of thread and tied it to two of my front teeth. Then she gave a big yank and that was that. When it was time for bed, she put them under my pillow and the next morning I got two nickels in their place. I'd also gotten hold of what Grandma called "an affliction." One week after going over to Miss Roberta Jean's house, Glory and I came down with the chicken pox. Turns out, Miss Roberta Jean had six kids who had just gotten over a recent bout two weeks earlier and were still contagious. We were covered in bumps and blisters "from tooth to toenail", is the way Grandma put it. I counted 184 bumps and Glory had 66. We had to take a bath every night in potato starch until they cleared up.

And I was growing faster than Jack's bean stalk. "Yo' feet is near 'bout as big as mine. I speck you'll be needing new shoes for school. It's gonna cost. God help us all," Grandma whispered as she struggled to fasten the strap across my foot. Glory had grown too. Her arms were way too long for her dresses. They stuck out like a turtleneck on a giraffe.

I also wondered about my father. *Is he still living in Chicago? Does he still live with my mother, and does she have any pictures of him?* I couldn't remember if I'd ever seen his face, and nobody ever said anything about him, except that he was a sergeant in the White man's army. When I asked Grandma about him, she said some things were best not mentioned. So I began to imagine. I imagined once he got out of the White man's army, he decided to seek more adventure out on the sea. He became a captain on a cargo ship that had set sail for the Indian Ocean, but had taken a wrong turn. The ship sank in a bad storm and he swam—with the help of kindly dolphins—to a nearby island inhabited by friendly but backward natives who made him king. But he was stranded there, with no radio or telephone and no way to reach the outside world. I mean, it was possible—I know, because I'd heard on the radio about something like that happening. I knew in my heart if my father thought I existed, and if he could escape off that island, he'd move heaven and earth to find me.

On the night before our trip, Grandma called for me to come sit on her lap by the black pot-bellied stove.

"How you feel 'bout goin' way up north?" Grandma asked.

"Well . . . I dunno. I guess it's all right."

"Is you at all scared?"

"Well . . . maybe, a little."

"It's okay to be afraid. But you ain't got to give in to fear. You know you gots a secret weapon."

"A weapon? What kind of weapon? And what I need it for?"

"Well suh, I guess you can call it a tiny mustard seed growing inside you . . . or—"

"Or a firefly? I swallowed one once."

"You say you ate 'em?"

"Yessum. Glory dared me to, but I think it's dead by now."

"Well, you in the presence of someone who can make things live again. Let's wake him up."

"Nooo! I don't wanna do that!"

"Listen, don't be scared, jus' have a little faith. When he wakes up, he ain't gonna be no ordinary firefly no more. No suh. Dis one here is gonna be special. And his light's gonna soar with the fierceness of fire, going into even the darkest of places! It's gonna burn and set ablaze any dangerous plots hiding beneath the surface of the wind. All you gotta do is keep his light turned on, and everything's gonna be fine."

"But . . . but where is this here firefly light, and how do I keep it turned on?"

"Haven't you felt his wings fluttering around inside yo' belly?"

"I don't think so. Well . . . maybe I have."

"Don't worry. I believe it's just been layin' there, patiently humming,

14

half asleep, right inside here." She patted my belly. "Now it's time to wake him up and let him fly 'round and 'round, till he goes right inside your heart. Now put your hand right here." She placed my hand over my heart. "You feel dat beatin' going on in there?"

"That's my heart," I said.

"Dat's where the firefly's gonna live. And when it comes time, he gonna move clear down to yo' belly for a signal. All right, um gonna pray for him to git stirred up."

She got down on her knees, placing both her hands over my heart, and began to pray, slowly at first, then so fast that I couldn't understand her words. As she prayed, it felt like the room was spinning, and what looked like a misty dew from a morning rain came in and covered her face. Then she touched my head lightly with one finger. "A double portion," she whispered. The room seemed to spin faster and I blacked out for a moment. I could still hear and know where I was, but it felt like I had drifted away and melted right into the misty dew.

Later that night, I lay awake in my bed. I tried to digest exactly what Grandma had said and done, but none of it made any sense because I couldn't feel anything stirring inside me. I looked under my bed to see if the firefly Grandma talked about was hiding under there. The only thing hiding there was a large, brown water bug. But I did feel a change had occurred. Something inside my body had shifted, but I couldn't figure out what. All I knew was I felt warm, happy, and safe, as if nothing in the world could ever harm me.

The next morning, Grandma dressed me and Glory in three layers of winter clothing. We wore long johns, T-shirts, dresses, pants, and snowsuits. She told us she wasn't taking any chances 'cause she had no idea how cold the temperature in Chicago would be in October.

"I done heard 'bout that Chicago flu and all dem city viruses making kids git the polio. If y'all witness anybody coughing, just cover your face wit yo' hands. Y'all hears me?"

"Yes, ma'am," we said.

When we got to the train station, I pulled Grandma away and whispered in her ear.

"Grandma, I been lookin' for that firefly and I ain't seen 'em nowhere."

"And you ain't gonna see him."

"Then he ain't really real, is he?"

"Things you cain't see is more real and true than things you can. You breathing air right now, but you cain't see it, can you? Don't you worry yo' head 'bout such things. You'll understand by and by."

Uncle Timmy ran over. "Train 'bout to take off, Mama. We gots to go."

As we boarded the train, Grandma gave us two big sacks of peanut butter and jelly sandwiches, fried chicken, and six large slices of 7Up cake. Then she gave us the biggest hugs of goodbye I'd ever had. "Now, Glory, you be sure to look after your little sister, you heah me?" She took out her hanky and wiped her eyes.

"Yes, ma'am," said Glory.

She turned to Uncle Timmy. "And make sure dey both get some sweet milk from the porter."

"Yes, ma'am," said Uncle Timmy.

Grandma gave us another looong hug and closed her eyes.

"Lord, bless these children and keep 'em safe," she prayed. Right then I suddenly realized that she wasn't coming with us. I mean, I knew it was only Glory and me going with Uncle Timmy, but I never stopped to digest the fact that we would be leaving Grandma behind. I held onto her as tightly as I could. I noticed Glory was holding on just as tight.

"Grandma, don't cry. We'll be back soon, won't we, Glory?" Glory never answered.

We took our seats on the massive Amtrak as it began its rumbling journey from the Texarkana station house. Miss Becky shared my seat, as I carefully placed her next to me. Glory squeezed her eyes shut and held onto the arms of the chair as the jerking train began to pick up speed. It was moving so quickly that sometimes we would bounce up and down in our seats like bunny rabbits. But I wasn't afraid. The excitement in my belly had come back as my thoughts turned again to what awaited me in the big city.

"Glory, did you know they gots indoor bathrooms with toilets that flush?"

"Yeah, so what?"

"And they gots hot and cold running water comin' right into the sink!"

"Yeah—so what?"

"And television!" Now, I had only seen television twice—once over my aunt Peggy's house and once when we went to downtown Texarkana. Big Ben's department store had set up a display window filled with RCA televisions. Glory and I just parked ourselves on the sidewalk and watched. That night I dreamed I was one of the Mouseketeers in the *Mickey Mouse Club*. I wore a Mickey Mouse hat and had long blonde pigtails. I held the hand of a boy named Eddie—it was written on the front of his shirt—who tried to take off my hat.

"Hey! You ain't a for real Mouseketeer!" Eddie said.

"Yes, I am. See, I've got mouse ears and everything. I even got blonde pigtails," I explained.

"Yeah, that's true. But you can't be a Mouseketeer."

"Why?"

"Because your skin is too black!"

That was when I woke up. I realized he was right. There were no Black Mouseketeers. But maybe, just maybe, I could be the first.

"I don't like television so much," Glory said, as she stared out the window. "I like listening to songs on the radio."

"Maybe one day you can sing on the radio and you can be famous!" I said, but she never replied. She just kept staring out the window.

After a while, I needed to go to the bathroom. "Glory—I have to go pee." She looked at me, then back out the window. I began moving around in my seat.

"I cain't hold it. I gotta go *now*!" I exclaimed.

Seeing my desperation, Glory looked around the train car, then at Uncle Timmy, who was reading a magazine, then back at me.

"Well . . . ask Uncle Timmy," she whispered. She held on tighter to the armrest and stared back out the window. It was obvious that she was not going to budge from her seat. I looked at Uncle Timmy, hoping he would take notice of me squirming around in my seat, but he was firmly focused on the pages in the magazine. When it came to paying attention to anyone's needs other than his own, he might need some coaxing.

I kicked him hard on his knee.

"I gots to go pee . . . now!"

Uncle Timmy looked up sharply, rubbing his knee. "Cain't you hold it 'til we gits to Chicago?"

"Nooooo! Me and Miss Becky gotta go now," I said, as I held onto my doll.

He looked around nervously for a woman to take us to the ladies' room but incredibly, the car was nearly empty. There were only a few men and an old woman who was sound asleep at the end of the car.

"Okay, come on. And Glory, you might as well come too." He jumped up, throwing his magazine down hard in his seat.

The train continued to jerk wildly as Glory and I held onto Uncle Timmy's hand. When we finally reached the ladies room in the next car, he pushed us forward.

"All right, go on in. Um not gonna go in wit you." After that, he turned and went back towards his seat.

Glory went in first. When she came out, I asked her to come in with me, but she refused. "I'll hold the door open so I kin see you. Now go ahead," she yelled over the screeching sounds of the locomotive engine.

Inside the bathroom, there was a big mirror on the wall, a sink, and a wooden toilet, which was just one big hole with a rim. I could actually see the tracks below as the train sped along. I held onto the toilet rim for dear life. As I looked down into the horrible hole and at the moving tracks, I had the strange feeling that I would be sucked in.

After I finished, I quickly jumped up. Then I tried to zip my snowsuit back up, but it was stuck. I looked at Glory to help me, but she suddenly released the door. It made a loud clanging noise as it slammed shut. *Had she closed it because it was too heavy or had she just got tired of holding it?* The train began to shake violently.

Still holding on to Miss Becky, I tried in vain again to zip up my snowsuit, but it just wouldn't budge. Pulling hard, I fell backwards, accidentally dropping Miss Becky into the horrible hole. There she was, stuck upside down, her head almost dragging on the tracks below while her dress was caught on a metal bolt that held the toilet down. I screamed, trying to pull her free. I became dizzy with fear as I ran to the door to get help, but I couldn't open it. It seemed to be locked from the outside. No matter how hard I pulled and turned the lock, it wouldn't open.

"Help! Glory . . . Somebody help me!" I screamed. I hoped that Glory could hear me, but she never answered. That's when I realized, she must have left me and walked back to her seat.

I longed to hear my grandmother's soothing voice telling me, *"Hush child, everything gonna be fine."* But instead I had to think quickly. *I have to save Miss Becky!* I yelled silently. Butterflies frantically fluttered around in my stomach, as I ran back to the toilet for one last effort. I leaned into the toilet hole headfirst, and grabbed and pulled with all my might. Suddenly, the bathroom door burst open. Uncle Timmy came flying in. He grabbed me by my legs and pulled me and Miss Becky to safety. That's when I realized superheroes don't always wear capes and masks.

I returned to my seat, and there sat Glory, eating a peanut butter and jelly sandwich. I wanted to ask her why she left me alone, and explain why she closed the door, but I said nothing and she said nothing. So for the rest of the two-day trip, we just sat quietly in our seats. We arrived in Chicago wet with pee, because neither of us would go back to the hole in the train. I wondered what my mother would think when she found out that all three layers of our clothing were totally soaked. But Miss Becky's grin was still intact. She only had a few black scuff marks across her face and a long tear in her dress as proof of her ordeal. Keeping her safe was the same as keeping all the memories of Grandma safe too. Like watching her hands as she carefully made Miss Becky—her smile was there too, along with her frown when I was misbehaving. I'd remember her eyes that never seemed to sleep—always watching, slow to anger and full of mercy. And now it would be up to me to be watchful over Miss Becky. I was going to make sure that no harm came to her while we were in the big city.

We took a long streetcar ride to my mother's apartment. It was hard trying to get all the suitcases on and off. When we got to the apartment, it looked like a very tired old man, wearing a crumpled gray and black suit. "302" was written in black on the concrete steps. We climbed all the way up three flights of stairs dragging our suitcases. Janetta Mae was waiting in the open doorway, wearing an orange flowery dress with matching orange lipstick. She was tall, thin, and brown-skinned. She wore a white flower in her black shiny hair that was piled high above her head. She didn't smile or frown. She just bit her bottom lip, and gave us all a puzzled gaze, as though this might be a dream.

After we'd taken off all our wet clothes and had some puffy cereal with milk, I realized that nothing was going to be like I had expected. There was only two rooms and a tiny kitchen. Glory and I would be sleeping on the let-out sofa in the living room.

Uncle Timmy told Janetta Mae, that this would be the last time he would ever travel with us again. But he never told her about what happened in the lady's bathroom. I think he didn't want Glory to get into any trouble for leaving me.

But I told. I told my grandma what happened when she called us on the big, black telephone in our hallway. I told how Uncle Timmy forgot to buy milk for us from the porter. And I told how Miss Becky fell down that horrible hole and how my uncle turned into a superhero. Then Grandma taught me a song right there on the spot so that I wouldn't be afraid of horrible holes. The song was called, *In That Hole*. She told me to repeat everything she said. Then Grandma started out by singing, "There was a hole—"

Then I said: "There was a hole."

Grandma: "It was the prettiest hole."

Me: "It was the prettiest hole."

Grandma: "Dat you ever did see."

Me: "Dat you ever did see."

Us: "Well, the hole in the ground, the green grass grew all around and around, the green grass grew all around."

♫ *And in dat hole, there was a tree. It was the prettiest tree, dat you ever did see.*
Well . . . the tree in the hole and the hole in the ground, green grass grew all around and around, the green grass grew all around. ♫

♫ *And on dat tree, there was a limb. It was the prettiest limb dat you ever did see.*
Well . . . the limb on the tree and the tree in the hole and the hole in the ground, the green grass grew all around and around, the green grass grew all around. ♫

22

♫ *And on the limb, there was a leaf. It was the prettiest leaf dat you ever did see.*

Well . . . the leaf on the limb and the limb on the tree and the tree in the hole and the hole in the ground, the green grass grew all around and around, the green grass grew all around. ♫

♫ *And on dat leaf, there was a nest. It was the prettiest nest dat you ever did see.*

Well . . . the nest on the leaf and the leaf on the limb and the limb on the tree and the tree in the hole and the hole in the ground, the green grass grew all around and around, the green grass grew all around. ♫

♫ *And in dat nest, there was an egg. It was the prettiest egg dat you ever did see.*

Well . . . the egg in the nest and the nest on the leaf and the leaf on the limb and the limb on the tree and the tree in the hole and the hole in the ground, the green grass grew all around and around, the green grass grew all around. ♫

♫ *And in dat egg, there was a bird. It was the prettiest bird, dat you ever did see.*

Well . . . the bird in the egg and the egg in the nest and the nest on the leaf and the leaf on the limb and the limb on the tree and the tree in the hole and the hole in the ground, the green grass grew all around and around, the green grass grew all around. ♫

♫ *And on dat bird, there was some feathers. It was the prettiest feathers, dat you ever did see.*

Well—the feathers on the bird and the bird in the egg and the egg in the nest and the nest on the leaf and the leaf on the limb and the limb on the tree and the tree in the hole and the hole in the ground, the green grass grew all around and around, the green grass grew all around. ♫

♫ *AND on them feathers, there was some colors. It was the prettiest colors, dat you ever did see.*

Well— (Deep breath) —the colors on the feathers and the feathers on the bird and the bird in the egg and the egg in the nest and the nest on the leaf and the leaf on the limb and the limb on the tree and the tree in the hole and the hole in the ground, the green grass grew all around and around, the green grass grew all around! ♫

CHAPTER 3

THE BIG CITY

Now that we had arrived in Chicago, everything took a lot of getting used to, especially the tall buildings, the loud radios, and the smell of smoky barbecue cooking on every street corner. Everyone talked way too fast and walked even faster. Janetta Mae would hold my hand tight, pulling me down the street. After a week I noticed that it was always hurry, hurry, hurry, even though we weren't late for anything. Our tired old building was filled with lots of noisy neighbors. Sometimes you could hear yelling coming from their apartments. But it was mostly crying babies that woke us up at night. However, we had a bathtub with hot and cold running water, an indoor toilet that flushed, and a new gas stove. But to my disappointment, we didn't have a television set. And there was even a bigger disappointment. Every day I'd sit and wait, hoping that my father would come by. I'd smile and look longingly into the faces of the men who came to our door only to find out that it was the milkman, or the mailman, or the landlord. Once, there was even a very short door-to-door salesman selling black pepper from a suitcase. He was nice, but he wasn't my daddy. Finally, I decided to just ask my mother.

"Janetta Mae, is my daddy ever gonna come by and see me, or is he still in the White man's army?"

"Army? Yo' daddy? Why you bothering me 'bout such things?"

"'Cause I wanna see him."

"Well, that ain't gonna happen. He's gone and that's that."

"Where's he gone? To a secret island in the Pacific?"

"What? Listen missy, I don't know where he is, and he don't know where I am, okay? And what did I tell you 'bout callin' me Janetta Mae?" She started dressing for work. I felt like I'd been hit in the face with a wet dishrag, but I kept pushing.

"Well uh . . . Uncle Timmy says you kin put ads in the newspaper and you kin find anybody, on account of everybody reads the newspaper. Kin we put an ad in the news—"

She stopped putting on her nylons. "Is you been listening to what I said? He gone and good riddance to bad rubbish! Last I seen him, he's 'sposed to buy me this diamond ring I seen in the storefront. He winds up bringin' me some ol' cheap gold band. I threw it back in his face and I ain't seen him since. Now, I gots to git to work."

After she had gone, I thought about what she'd said long and hard. I thought about her wanting me to call her mama, and I thought about what she said about my daddy. That's when I made a vow to find him. When I got old enough, I vowed, I would put an ad in every newspaper in Chicago . . . as soon as I figured out what his first and last name was. And I made a vow never to call her mama.

Today was a special day. Janetta Mae had a day off from work and she was taking Glory and me to Woolworth's—the five-and-dime store for school supplies. We bought pencils and lined notebook paper, crayons in sixteen different colors, white paste, erasers, and leather satchels. Tomorrow, Glory and I would register at Benjamin Banneker Elementary School. Glory was in fourth grade and I was in second.

Janetta Mae walked quickly down the street as she talked. We ran to keep up with her. "Now Glory, it's gonna be up to you to make your way home with Sandy after school. I don't git off work till five o'clock, so I won't be home till six. I'm gonna leave some sandwiches in the ice box and all y'all have to do is wait in the house till I git home. I'm gonna give you my spare key and you better not lose it or you gonna be locked outside in the dark. You understand what I said?"

"Yessum," Glory said. The familiar look of fear starts to bathe her face in gloomy shadows. She hated being scolded, so she tried hard not to make mistakes.

The next morning when Janetta Mae woke us up for school, it was still dark outside. We had oatmeal, which I hated, and cheese toast, which I loved, for breakfast. As we got ready to leave the house, I put Miss Becky into my leather book satchel.

"Where you going with that doll?" Janetta Mae asked.

"She going wit me to school. I—"

"Listen here missy. She ain't going nowhere. A doll ain't got no place at school. You goin' there to learn, not to play." She quickly removed Miss Becky and threw her on the couch. I wanted to kick her, to scream at her, *You can't tell me what to do. You ain't my real mother! Grandma's my real mother!* Those words were ready to pour out like angry bees from a honeycomb, but I didn't say anything because I knew Grandma wouldn't like it.

The school building was battered, dreary, and neglected. It had tall, chipped, limestone pillars in front with a chain-linked fence surrounding it. There was black, red, and yellow graffiti written on everything. The closer we came, the worse it looked. As we climbed the stairs, I began to shiver, even though it was quite warm for late October.

Janetta Mae took me to my classroom and just left me there. As I looked at all the new faces gathered in one big room, I wanted to run. I looked back to see if by some miracle my mother had returned, but all I saw was the unfamiliar face of my teacher. She wore large, round glasses, bright pink lipstick, and a gentle smile. I smiled back a little inside. As she bent

28

down, she quickly took the handkerchief from her pocket and wiped the tears from my face.

Illustration by Marlon Hall

"Hello, Sandy. My name is Miss Jefferson, and I'm very glad you're here." She took me by the hand and introduced me to everyone in the class. Then she showed me where to hang my coat and what desk I would be sitting at. A girl wearing glasses sitting in front of me turned around and poked out her tongue.

At recess, the older girls played a game called *hopscotch,* in an area where they had drawn squares with colored chalk. Other girls made up funny rhymes as they jumped together in a rope called *double-dutch.* I watched closely to learn the rules, hoping one day I might be asked to play. A small-framed girl with red hair and freckles came over to me. She took my hand and led me to the school steps.

"You can play with me," she said. She took out a tiny, red ball and a handful of little silver stars from her pocket.

"What's yo' name?" I asked. She didn't answer.

"Mine's Sandy and I's from Texas."

"You talk funny. Does everybody talk like that where you from?"

"I 'spect so."

"Well you're not in Texas now, so you better learn how to talk proper English," she said.

"Okay. Kin you teach me?"

"I guess so," she said reluctantly. "But now I'm going to teach you the game of *Jacks*."

After a lunch of strange meat sandwiches and milk, all the girls had to go to the gymnasium for what Miss Jefferson called, PE. Everyone changed into gym shoes and blue shorts except me. Mrs. Jefferson told me I could sit on the bench until it was over.

When we were getting ready to go home, Mrs. Jefferson told me to wait at her desk.

"Sandy, when you go home, can you remember to let your mother know you will need a white pair of sneakers and a pair of blue gym shorts?"

"Well, yessum, but we already did our shopping for school supplies yesterday, and my mama said that was all we was gonna git."

"Okay . . . What I'll do is send a note home with you to your mother." Then she wrote a note and pinned it on the front of my jacket.

After I left my class, I stood outside in the schoolyard and waited for Glory. Tall boys and girls ran past me into the courtyard. They were pushing and shoving and cussing at each other. I tried to make out Glory's face among the crowd, but it was useless. Finally, after everyone had left, and the schoolyard was nearly empty, I realized I had to make a decision.

I climbed the steps to the school entrance and pushed on the doors but they were locked. I sat on the steps for a while, hoping that Glory would return. I could hear my grandma's voice in my head singing, *Jesus loves the little children— They won't have to fear. Jesus loves the little children because they are so dear.*

Next, something happened that I didn't figure on. It began to get dark. That's when I knew that I had better try to make it back home on my own. I closed my eyes and made a wish that my grandma would suddenly appear, taking my hand in hers. But when I opened them, she wasn't there.

Then, in the back of my mind, a picture came up, like a map, showing me street after street of where I had walked. I began to walk, following the map in my head. Amazingly, I saw the numbers 302 painted on my steps. Even though I wasn't quite sure what our address numbers were, I knew that the picture of them in my mind was the same. I had gotten home just as the streetlights came on.

When I came inside, Glory was crying, and Janetta Mae looked worried. She still had on her white uniform from work.

"You better stop crying befo' I give you something to cry about," she said to Glory. Then she turned and saw me standing inside the doorway. "Girl! I was just about to come up to that school. How did you git home?" she asked, closing the door.

"I came home by myself. I remembered where we lived. I was kinda scared but—"

"Well, you home now. And I don' told Glory she better not ever come back here without you, else she gonna get the beatin' of her life. What's that pinned on your coat?"

"My teacher, Miss Jefferson, said I need gym shoes and shorts, so she give me this note for you. She said I—"

Janetta Mae didn't wait for me to finish. She just snatched the note from my coat and read it. Then she started talking to herself real low, like the whispers through ceiling boards at my grandma's house. She walked into her bedroom and closed the door.

31

"Why didn't you look for me after school?" I asked.

"I guess I forgot."

"You forgot? It got dark and you wasn't even—"

"I had a lot of things to remember," Glory interrupted. "I won't forget tomorrow."

This was the second time that Glory had simply forgotten me. It made me feel like she was more of an enemy than my closest friend. Because I figured that you could forget a pencil or a book, or even a pet, but it was really hard to forget a person, especially a friend.

CHAPTER 4

ENOUGH IS ENOUGH!

Janetta Mae liked to go out dancing on Saturday nights with her two best friends, Clara Mae and Thelma. When they'd be getting ready, Thelma would play loud blues music on the stereo and pop her fingers. They would put on lots of red nail polish, matching lipstick, and lime-green eye shadow. They wore shiny silver-sequined dresses and teased their hair so high they could barely get under the overhanging archway. Looking at them made me wonder: *What did dressing up like a neon sign at night have to do with dancing?*

Sometimes our *"cousins"* would babysit us. They were not our real cousins, they were the children of Clara Mae and Thelma. Out of the nine children, I never knew who belonged to whose mother. They made us do things that we couldn't tell anybody about. Like when they took us to the store and got us to steal things, or—putting candy in their pockets while we pretended to talk with the shop owner. And when we got back to their house, they would threaten us with their fists if we told anyone. It was like being thrown in a tank with hungry, man-eating sharks. The only way to survive was to swim and I hadn't learned yet.

I had no regard for any of them, except one little boy. His name was Sam, but everyone just called him Foster Kid. Sam couldn't talk or walk. He'd just sit in his wheelchair staring out the window. At first I would stand

33

at a far distance, just close enough to watch him twitching his hands back and forth. But whenever I came nearer, he'd give me the biggest smile. And the closer I came the happier he got. He'd almost fall out of his chair jumping around so much.

"Can you guess what's in my hand?" I asked as I balled up both fists.

"Un-un," he grunted.

"Pick!" He put his hand over my left fist and I opened it. Inside I had one green bubblegum. He let out a big screaming laugh and I gave it to him. But the cousins were not happy at all to see us having so much fun. A tall, angry looking girl named Teeny came over and stared at us.

"He cain't have no gum 'cause he'll choke." She took the gum from his hand and popped it into her mouth and began chewing, blowing big bubbles.

On another *"visit"* to the cousins, they were ready to strike. Because just like all sharks, when they smelled blood, they attacked. When Janetta Mae bought Glory and me new panties with pink ruffles, one of the older girls, named Huckabuck, saw them and made us take them off. Huckabuck hung them out the window on a long broom handle and threatened to drop them. We yelled and screamed until she stopped laughing and gave them back to us. We never wore the ruffled panties to their house again.

Finally, after almost a year of being in the big city, I'd had enough. It was now 1961, and I was tired of all the noisy police sirens and loud music that played day and night. I was tired of being left with the cousins who stole our panties and beat the back of our hands with playing cards to teach us how to play by the rules. And most of all, I'd had enough of the smells of the city with its crumbling concrete buildings surrounded by trash and broken liquor bottles.

Illustration by Marlon Hall

I missed the tall trees, green grass, and the red dirt of Texas. I wanted to go back home to my grandmother and smell her biscuits and ham baking in the kitchen. And even though our apartment had an indoor toilet with hot and cold water faucets, and Janetta Mae had bought us a new black-and-white television and we could watch all the cartoons we wanted on Saturdays, I was still unhappy. I felt so out of place like a snowfall in August. I was sure Glory felt the same way, but my silent sister never said anything. She would just sit on the floor in the corner reading her comic books. So one day, I felt it was time to open my big mouth. I decided to ask Janetta Mae to let us go back home. She and Glory were at the sink washing dishes.

"Janetta Mae, it was real nice you lettin' us come and visit and all, but can we please go back home now?"

"What did I say 'bout callin' me Janetta Mae? I'm yo' mama and you needs to call me Mama," she said, throwing her dish cloth in the sink. "Glory calls me mama, why don't you?"

"If I promise to call you mama will you take us back to Texas?"

"What you talkin' 'bout?" she whispered.

"Well . . . *Mama* . . . me and Glory wanna go back home. Please, ma'am," I said softly.

"Well missy, this is yo' home now. Both you and Glory. So you better git used to it." I didn't think I could do that, but the look in her eyes said I'd better try.

"Fine. I'll start callin' you mama if you stop callin' me missy!" I said, and stormed into the bathroom locking the door.

"Fine!" Mama yelled from the other side.

A few weeks later, the Dixie Cup factory closed down, and now my mama was out of a job. With no money, she couldn't keep up with the monthly rent and expenses. She borrowed money from her friend Thelma for three train tickets, and just like that, we were headed back to Hooks. When Mama told us the news, I started jumping around like a bullfrog in a West Texas hailstorm. Glory didn't say anything as usual. She just gazed solemnly out the window watching the traffic below. Then she reached under the bed and pulled out both of our suitcases. Finally, a tiny smile passed over her face, and the clouds of despair she lived under seemed to evaporate.

On the day we were to leave, we packed our suitcases and Mama packed her big trunk. But there was something missing: Miss Becky. She had been hiding for three days! Just before summer vacation, I had stuck her under my sweater and taken her to school to show her off to my teacher and all the kids. Later that evening Kiki came over to my house to play with me and Miss Becky. She was the same girl who'd taught me how to play Jacks on the first day of school. She said Miss Becky was the prettiest doll she had ever seen. That had been three days ago and I hadn't seen Becky since. At first I didn't think about it. But now we were leaving and she was still nowhere to be found. I looked everywhere and in every corner of the house.

Glory had even tried to help me look. She climbed up to shelves I couldn't reach and crawled under Mama's big bed, but it was hopeless.

"Okay, that's it," Mama said. "When we git to Texas, Mama will make you another doll. You cain't—"

"No. I'm not leavin' without my doll. I know she's—"

"I'm gonna give you five more minutes. Now, do you understand?" Mama's tone had turned from promises to perils.

I ran faster, looking around the house again. Five minutes, ten minutes . . . now I really needed that firefly. *Where was he?* I'd hoped that his light would guide me to where Miss Becky was, but there was nothing, not even a whisper. Was the firefly real or just some fable Grandma told me so I wouldn't be afraid?

Finally my mother said enough was enough and we had to go without Miss Becky. But I couldn't leave her behind. Having searched the entire house and turned up nothing, all I could do was sit on the floor and cry.

"Come on. Git up off that floor! You ain't fixin' to make us miss our train on account of no doll."

"Noooo! Um not gonna go without Becky!"

"That's it!" she said, and picked me up kicking and screaming. She carried me to the taxi waiting outside. I squeezed my eyes shut, trying to block out the image of Miss Becky lying in some dark place, just waiting for me to find her. She would think I had abandoned her. I didn't want to imagine the sad look in her eyes when she realized we'd never see each other again.

As we pulled out of the Union train station, the rain fell hard, beating against the windows, matching the tears in my eyes. I sat next to Glory, and I wanted to bite her until she bled. Her doll, who she never even bothered to name, was safely tucked away in her suitcase. I wondered again about this firefly that Grandma had said would help me when I needed him. How come he didn't light up the place where Becky was hiding? Maybe I needed to learn how to make this firefly work. But how? Like wet from water, my anger began to pour out. I was angry at the train for taking me away from Becky. I was angry at Uncle Timmy for bringing me here in the first place. And I was mad at Kiki, who just might have taken Becky out of envy, and I was especially angry at Janetta Mae for making me call her *Mama* when I didn't really want to. But most of all I was angry at myself for not taking care of Miss Becky the way I should have. She depended on me and I had let her down.

Suddenly Glory turned to me, giving me her handkerchief. "Don't you worry 'bout Miss Becky," she said. "She gonna be all right. Grandma made her outta strong materials. And she's real pretty. So you kin bet, iffin anybody find her, they gonna take care of her jus' like you did. And you know what? Um thinkin' um too old to be playin' wit dolls. So you kin play wit mine iffin you want. I know she ain't anything like Miss Becky, but she do need somebody to play wit her and take care of her, like you."

She took her doll out of her suitcase and carefully placed her in my arms. The adoption was complete and so was the forgiveness. I forgave Glory for leaving me in the schoolyard. I forgave her for leaving me alone with the horrible hole on the train and for all the other acts of unkindness I had kept a record of since the silence had begun. And I was glad that on this night, she had decided to share both her doll and her words with me.

I could only hope Miss Becky found a nice home and a kind person to take care of her. And even though my firefly hadn't chosen to show his light, Glory had chosen to speak to me—to find her voice. Perhaps this was the beginning of unlocking the secret to her silence, if only for a moment. Maybe that was the plan all along. The firefly must have known it would take a big sacrifice to get my sister back and he was willing to sacrifice Miss Becky. Now wasn't that just like a real friend?

CHAPTER 5

FIREFLIES

dreams and fireflies wander 'bove my head
how can fireflies live and dreams be dead
like dreams, dey comes to me at night
by mornin' dey gone and taken flight
taking summers light, in winter dey go
such a pretty sight, like heaven's afterglow
how dey git so bright , I'll never know
now as I lay me down and ponder,
if what I dream ain't real
din I jus' hold onto the wonder,
and all the hope I feel

Crickets were having some kind of a party, dancing and singing in the grass outside my window. Their music was keeping me awake. One song kept time with my heartbeat as I lay there—still. The bed was damp with my sweat. I waited for a breeze to wander in, but it never came. As I wiped the palms of my hands on the clean, crisp white linen, I heard whispering from the next room. My fingers felt for the creases in the sheet. It testified of the strength my grandmother used when she ironed, pressing down hard until the edge of each pleat could cut you. I was now at peace. I was home. The exasperating, two day journey on the Amtrak train was now just a memory.

"All aboard, ma'am! Bound for Texarkana, Texas. All aboard ma'am! All aboard!" the conductor yelled, as he lifted me up and onto the platform. At one in the morning, I'd lost my little red coin purse, changing trains in St. Louis. Mama said we couldn't stop to look.

Now that we had finally arrived, I felt I could breathe again and Chicago had no more claims to me. I knew I never wanted to leave my grandmother's house again. I never ever wanted to go back—there.

The sounds were getting louder in the next room. Now, I could make out the voices of Mama and Grandma. Their conversation drifted, like incense through the paper-thin walls of the tiny three-room cottage.

"Well, I sho' hope you can look after the kids for a while. You know, not jus' for the summer—maybe they can start school too. It's kinda hard tryin' to find employment with them two hangin' 'round my neck," Mama said.

"Well now, look here. I don't mind tending to Glory," Grandma said as carefully as she could. "But Sandy . . . dat girl is too headstrong. She don't be minding me. You know, I started volunteering on Saturdays at the church and—"

"You gotta keep 'em both, 'cause I ain't got no money for a sitter, and I caint jus' leave 'em in the house alone. People gits into lots of trouble for things like that," Mama whispered.

"Well . . . I speck I'll think on it awhile. I don't want to see you git in no kinda trouble. But it's gonna be real hard to stretch my sixty-dollars-a-month Security check to feed two more mouths—"

"Now Mama, you know 'umma be sending you some money every month soon as I'm able," she insisted with renewed hopefulness. "And where did Timmy run off to? Ain't he still working at the grain factory and helpin' out around here?"

"I thought I had wrote to you dat he done gone and joined up with the army . . . no, I think it was the marines. Said he'd had enough of that factory with slave wages. Well, I sure do miss him. I sure do."

I closed my eyes. A beautiful peace overwhelmed me. We were all together again, except for Uncle Timmy. Tomorrow I would scrub the grime and dirt of Chicago's tenement ghettos off me. It had gotten clean under my fingernails and into the roots of my hair. *Tomorrow, umma get clean,* I thought. I'd use the Ivory soap that Grandma always kept in the bottom cupboard shelf. And I'd take a bath in the big metal wash tub that hung outside the back porch. Tomorrow I would skip down the dirt road, until I reached Aunt Hattie's house and sip sweet tea under her big shade tree. I'd have all summer to swing on the rope behind the smokehouse and chase chickens, catch fireflies, and do whatever seven year old girls did when they entered paradise, after being in hell.

The next morning the old rooster woke me up just as he'd always done, and Grandma was making eggs and grits just like I'd remembered so many times before. I closed my eyes and quickly opened them to make sure it wasn't a dream.

A week had passed, and it was a beautiful summer's night in late June. There were thousands of fireflies lighting up the night sky in my grandmother's front yard. They'd all came back, just like I remembered. It reminded me how much Glory and I *loved* chasing them. At night, we would catch them and put them on our ears to make glow-in-the-dark earrings. Earlier, we'd stolen empty glass mason jars from the smokehouse and filled them with as many as we could. Glory tried to make a hole in the lid of hers with a pocket knife, but it slipped, shattering her jar in pieces.

"Gimme!" Glory yelled, as she tried to snatch away my mason jar.

"No way. It's mine!" I yelled back. I held on tight as she tried to twist my arm.

Grandma heard all the yelling and came outside to see what was going on. "Now, Sandy, what you fussin' bout? You behave yo'self before I have to git my switch!"

"But, Grandma, Glory tryin' to take my jar 'cause hers broke!"

"All right, that's enough of dis foolishness. Come on in heah, the both of you and gits ready fo' bed."

"Yes ma'am!" we said in unison.

We knew to obey when she put both hands on her hips because the next thing she would get was her switch. Now a switch was a long, thin branch from a tree. She would find the sturdiest branch and remove all the leaves with one swift hand. Then she would hold me over her knee and count out at least ten lashes while she administered the punishment.

The next few weeks came and went. There were no sad ceremonies. No thunderstorm, hail, no cooling of the sun. It still beat down hot and fast into my magnifying glass as I lay in the sand killing ants. As twilight came and night overshadowed us, I gazed up at the brilliance of the stars and wondered why the universe didn't get angry and just turn off its light, letting the blackness cover everything. But it didn't happen. Mama's decision to leave didn't even stop the fireflies. They still gave off their green florescent glow as I gathered them into my mason jar.

"Don't die, don't die," I whispered. "You better not, or I ain't never gonna take care of you no more." I closed the lid tightly, so none would escape. I hid them under my bed, and came back out on the porch.

Mama sat in a rocking chair on the front porch waiting for Uncle Billy to come with his shiny black Ford car. She wore her cat-eye sunglasses even though it was now dark, and her pink poodle skirt with white pearls and a flowery shirt. Her hair was pulled back into a long ponytail. With chocolate-brown skin and the delicate poise of an icy statue, she was pleasingly perfect.

Mama's older brother, Uncle Zippy, sat on a wooden crate at the opposite end of the porch, spitting liquid black snuff into an old coffee can. He had come to bid Mama a fond farewell before she left for Chicago. His real name was Edward, but they called him Zippy for fun because he moved around like a turtle. He even drove his car well below the actual speed limit. I heard that people on bikes were actually passing him while giving him a wave, which was why Mama was getting a ride from Uncle Billy.

One time when he was driving me, Glory, and Grandma to church, I decided to get to know more about Uncle Zippy.

"Uncle Zippy, why you drive so slow?"

"Well—baby girl, it's like dis here. White patrol officers for the most part is all right, but they gits real nervous and surprised when they sees colored folks driving up and down the highways. They start to wonder where in God's speed we is all goin'. So I drives my car jus' slow enough so they kin see the smile on Uncle Zippy's face. Then I wave . . . That unarms 'em to the point where they gits familiar with who I am. So, um just standing at my post, doing my part to keep 'em from gettin' upset with unnecessary wondering."

You see, Uncle Zippy was either the smartest man I'd ever met or the craziest. He was always saying things that took all of my imagination to understand, like—"It's more than one way to skin a cat." *But why would anyone want to do that?* Or—"Jus' because you sees a mountain don't mean you have to climb it. Resist it instead." *Hmmm . . . now what exactly did that mean?*

Mama gave Uncle Zippy a big hug. "I'm gonna miss you, Zippy," she said.

"Well, little sister, um gonna wait a little while, then um gonna miss you too," he replied, as he spat another glob of snuff into the can.

I couldn't make up my mind if I agreed with Uncle Zippy about waiting a while before I would miss Mama or if I would even miss her at all. All I thought about when I was in Chicago was leaving. Now I felt confused. Was it the city I wanted to leave, or was it my mother? I didn't know what it would feel like living in Texas with my mother. Maybe things would be different. Maybe . . .

"Mama, when you comin' back?" I said, hugging her around the waist.

She pulled my hands away and straightened her skirt. "I'll be back as quick as you can say 'jack rabbit'. "

"But that's a lie, 'cause I can say 'jack rabbit' and you still be leaving."

Grandma came on the porch and pulled my ponytail hard. "Sandy, don't you ever call yo' mama a liar. You heah me?"

"And what if she is? What if she ain't never told the truth? What if she ain't never comin' back?"

Grandma pulled my ponytail harder. "You see how she talkin' back to me? She says the first thing that comes to her mind. That's one reason right heah that I knows it's gonna be trouble."

I tried to wiggle away from Grandma's death grip. "Lemme go! Grandma, will you just listen—"

"Baby girl," Uncle Zippy interjected. "Now you jes settle down. Don't fill up yo' mouth with all *you* know. Leave some room for what you don't." He winked at me as he took out a nickel from the pocket of his worn overalls and slipped it into my hand.

It seemed like Grandma had grown weary of all my questions and loud talk. Since I'd been away, her patience had gotten as thin as the pages in her Bible.

"Listen," Mama said, ignoring Uncle Zippy. "I gotta go look for work, but I'll be back real soon, you'll see. You just be good and mind your grandmother. You understand me?"

"Yes, ma'am," I said. Grandma finally loosed me as I leaned towards my mother to give her a kiss. But as usual, she turned away, and held my hands down again.

"Stop meddlin' around. You gonna mess me all up."

"But, Mama, why can't you live here? Why can't we all live here together with Grandma?"

"In this old, broken-down shack? You'd have to pay me to live in this town."

Right at that very moment, the tiny hope of us all being happy together vanished. Her idea of home was as far away from mine as a desert from the ocean. Where I saw a cottage filled with love, she saw an old, broken down shack. Miss Becky was not something to treasure but to abandon, the way she was abandoning us . . . again. And although I would call her Mama, in my heart she would always be *Janetta Mae*.

"Glory! Come on out heah and give yo' Mama a big hug. I heah Uncle Billy's Ford a-comin'," Grandma called inside as she put her fists to her hips.

Glory slowly opened the torn screen door. She came toward Mama, her head hung low. I couldn't tell if she was sad to see Mama go or just had her usual depressed look. I remembered when she won first place at Talent Round Up when she sang, *"Mama's Lil' Baby like Shortnin' Bread"*. As they were clapping and handing her the trophy, all she did was stare down at her feet. No, I didn't know of anything that made her show real happiness. Not even Christmas candy canes, or fuzzy toy chicks, or fireflies, or . . .

"My fireflies!" I screamed. I ran inside the house to check the mason jar that I had hid under my bed away from Glory. I shook it again and again. They were dead all right. I took the jar outside and dumped them into the backyard.

Glory came out back and stood beside me. "So they died," she said.

"Yep," I answered.

"I figured they would. That's why I was gonna put holes in the jar, but you wouldn't let it go. I was gonna give it back you know. You better come on in and say goodbye to Mama. She fixin' to leave with Uncle Billy." She took my hand.

We came back to the front porch to find Mama giving Grandma a hug. The black Ford was parked in the front yard. Uncle Billy leaped out of his massive car, leaving the lights on and the door open. He was short, round and shirtless, wearing overalls and smoking a hand-rolled cigarette. He was also married to Mama's sister, Auntie Pearl. Sweat dripped off his forehead as he climbed up on the porch. Taking off his farmers' cap, he bowed to everyone.

"Well, here he is," Grandma whispered. "Cigarette fire on one end, fool on the other."

"How do, Miss Minnie Bell . . . Zippy . . . How do, Janetta Mae . . . kids?" Uncle Billy growled.

"We's all doin' jus' fine, Billy," Grandma said.

"Well, Pearl couldn't make it out 'cause she was busy cookin' up that hog meat for tomorrow. You see, we is fixin' to have that big preacher from Dallas and his family over our house for dinner. Just bought a twelve-piece dining room set with velvet cushions and everythin' just so he'll have plenty of room to relax."

"Is that right?" Grandma said, tapping her feet.

"Yes, ma'am. But she sho' wanted to come out to send her sister back to Chicago. We's fixin' to take a vacation with the kids to—"

"Ain't you best to be getting Janetta Mae to the station house? Train be comin' soon," Grandma said.

"Well, you is right about that. Come on, Zippy, let's load her up. But best be careful now. This here car cost a pretty penny. Don't wanna damage somethin' you cain't pay for."

Grandma sighed as she folded her arms. "I guess that makes two of y'all," she mumbled.

Uncle Billy and Uncle Zippy both struggled as they loaded Mama's worn travel trunk and leather suitcase into the trunk of the car.

Glory gave Mama another little hug, being careful not to get too close. Then she quietly came over and held my hand again. As we both stood there together holding hands, our silence spoke of shared memories. Grandma said Mama was only nineteen when Glory was born. Maybe she had been too young. It was almost like we were all growing up together and finding out about what it meant to love. Because how could she teach us what she herself was still learning?

Before Uncle Billy pulled off, taking Mama away to the train station, he waved to us to come over to the window. He reached his hand out. "Open your hands. Here's a quarter each. Git yourselves some sweets tomorrow, and remember it was your Uncle Billy dat rewarded you."

"Thanks, Uncle Billy," we said in unison. Then he threw out his cigarette and pulled away.

I ran after the car yelling, "Jack rabbit! Jack rabbit!" and waving, not sure if I would ever see Mama again. But she never looked back. The red dust from the road was all that was left to testify of her departure. I put my hands over my eyes so I wouldn't see—over my ears so I wouldn't hear the noise of the sirens in my head pronouncing, "*She's dead, she's dead!*" when they saw the condition of my soul.

Then came the fireflies—millions of them swarming above my head. My heart beat faster as I realized my very own firefly that had been recreated to comfort me, had called them down. Their spirits were indestructible. They, too, seemed to have been reborn even more glorious than before. And so was I reborn, not of flesh and blood, but of hope and faith—invisible things that my grandmother had talked about. I felt my soul would survive after all. It would be renewed in the life of the firefly.

Glory came down the road holding the mason jar. She had poked holes in the lid with a knife. "They kin breathe now," she said as she handed it to me. I looked up in awe at the glowing creatures and I heard a voice speaking from my heart—

"I'll take good care of you, I promise," my firefly whispered as tears streamed down my face. "I'll keep watch while you sleep. I'll light up in dark closets, finding the keys to your daydreams, while locking up dragonflies and centipedes that hide in your nightmares. My wings were made to carry you over narrow bridges, murky waters, and lonely deserts. Can't you feel the warmth of my glow? The joy of my promise? Or the song of my praise?"

♫ *This little light of mine, I'm gonna let it shine. This little light of mine, I'm gonna let it shine. Let it shine, let it shine, let it shine . . .* ♫

Illustration by Marlon Hall

CHAPTER 6

TALE OF TWO SNAKES

iffin' too much sweets gon' make me ill
din feed me chocolate against my will
and take me down to the candy sto'
buy me Baby Ruth's, Mint Juleps and mo'
gonna wash it all down wit lime soda pop
maybe a red snow cone jus' 'cause it's hot
and tell the doctor iffin' I gits ill
jus' gimme a lil' water and a sugar pill

The August heat in our small town of Hooks was relentless. The only activity that late afternoon in 1962 was a throng of lazy green flies converging around our outhouse. I finally sought refuge on my grandmother's back porch. I lay there in the swing with my head back, eyes closed, dreaming of being carried on a barge down the Nile River by Egyptian slaves, or flying in a hot air balloon over the Andes Mountains. And then like magic, I'd find myself in the back of a Dairyland ice cream truck. Sometimes if I tried hard enough, I could even taste big helpings of the smooth chocolate and cold caramel ice cream melting in my mouth, crunchy, brown sugary cones made of thin wafery—

"Boo!"

Startled, I opened my eyes. Standing over me was a very dirty little

boy with chubby cheeks and buckteeth. He grinned down at me, dangling a
dead caterpillar inches from my nose.

"Leroy! Leroy, I hate you," I said. Rising from the swing, I swatted
the caterpillar to the ground.

"No you don't."

"Yes I do!"

"No you don't!" he said, wiping the mud from his dirty hands onto
his T-shirt. He then put his hand in one pocket and pulled it out. He was
holding something in his tight little fist.

"Betcha cain't guess what I got in my hand." His grin was getting
wider.

"Betcha I don't even care!" I turned my back to him, pretending to
look at dragonflies dancing on the screen door.

"I'll give you five guesses," he said.

I turned around sharply, physically holding my hand down from hitting him. "Leroy, will you jus'—"

"Lookee here!" he squealed. It didn't seem as though he cared one bit that he was inches away from being punched in the face. He slowly opened his hand to reveal a small object. "It's a real rattler of a for-real rattlesnake! My mama cut his tail clean off!"

"You're lyin!" I yelled.

"Am not!"

"Are too!"

"Am not!" He stomped his foot defiantly, putting his fists to his side as he rolled his eyes. Looking at his expression, I realized it was useless to try and out-yell him, so I would have to invent another path to go down.

"Leroy, how old is you?"

"I dunno." He shrugged his shoulders as he gazed up at the cloudless sky.

"You don't know how old you is? Boy, jus' like I figured, you is pretty stupid."

"Am not! Um old enough to know what I done seen."

"You think uma gonna believe yo' crazy mama cut that off a live rattlesnake? You're not only stupid, you're a liar too. My grandma says all liars go to hellfire."

"I is not a liar! And my mama's not crazy. She cut that snake's head clean off wit the ax when we found it in the smokehouse the other day. And then she cut off the rattler tail. Mama says it's for protection against haints and demons and such. And I was fixin' to give it to ya' for a present. Now I's not gonna give you nothin' on account you callin' me a liar." He put the rattler back into his pocket.

Having babies and dipping snuff was all I'd seen his mother, Mellie Bee, do without practice. I couldn't imagine her handling anything as big as an ax. I'd heard Grandma say to somebody that she'd went half-crazy three years ago when her husband, Nathan Bee, left her and their four kids for a fast-talking, hip-twistin' woman from Dallas. Eventually, they said Mellie Bee stopped bathing or even combing her hair. She never came out of her house, even to go to church. That's why on most Sunday nights Grandma brought church to her. Grandma would come over with food and her big white Bible. But Mellie Bee would just take the food and refuse the Bible study.

I jumped off the porch and got directly in Leroy's face. "Mama say this and Mama say that. What yo' mama knows could fit inside a teaspoon. Besides . . . Grandma says you ought to have respect for living things— murderer. And you smell like a dead skunk!" I yelled, backing away.

Leroy's beaver cheeks hung down like two brown deflated sacks. A tiny pang of guilt beat in my eight-year-old heart for just a fraction of a second. I mean, he was the product of silly Mellie Bee and cheating Nathan Bee. I didn't think he was worth too much of my sympathy.

"And you as mean as that ol' rattlesnake!" he said, holding back tears.

"Oh, go to hell, Leroy! And while you there, ask the devil to make you some bath water, dirty duck butt!"

"Ooooh. You cussed! You said the H-word! Umma tell yo' grandma on you."

"*Hell* ain't no cuss word. I hears the preacher say it all the time. Now shut up and git off my porch before I—" I pinched him hard on his arm.

Crying, Leroy jumped off the porch and ran into the woods. "Dirty duck butt!" I yelled after him.

"Sandy? Yoo-hoo, *Saanndy!* You out thare?" Grandma called to me from the kitchen. "Well, I say, thare you are! Come on in heah. You gots a pretty, young lady caller waitin' on you," she cooed. Her voice dripped with Southern hospitality.

Peering through the backdoor, I could see ten-year-old Peggy Lomax sitting on our worn-out sofa. Her hands folded with ladylike dignity. Her blue-checkered dress was perfectly pleated. Two blue-and-white bows were tied to her carefully plaited ponytails. My dislike for her was immediate. I had met Peggy only once before when we were both asked to recite a verse in front of the church for Easter. We were supposed to hold hands together and bow, but she refused and had put her hand behind her back instead.

Now, I sadly stared down at my dirty, unwashed feet, cut-off jeans, and T-shirt. I wanted to run, but it was too late. Grandma opened the screen door and pulled me inside. Awkwardly, I moved toward the living room. Grandma excused herself to the front porch.

"Hi, Sandy, y'all want to see my new bike?" said Peggy. I watched, as she batted away a fly that dared to enter her sacred space.

"Hi, Peggy."

"Well?"

"Well what?"

"Come on, I know you want to ride it. Don't 'cha?"

"You mean yo' bike? I . . . uhh, I can't, I uhh . . ."

"Well, I'm gonna ride over to Mr. Parker's store and buy some stuff. Y'all wanna go too?"

"I ain't got my allowance yet," I lied.

"Well, silly, why don't y'all git it from yo' grandmother? We kin be the first ones to try out that Laffy Taffy candy. It's real nice since Mr. Parker took over. Go on, ask Miss Minnie Bell for a nickel."

I ventured out to the front porch, knowing full well I'd never gotten an allowance. But the picture of the candy store had suddenly appeared in my mind with amazing clarity. I could almost smell the ginger snaps and raspberry coolies.

"Uhhh . . . Grandma, you got a nickel?" I asked softly, hoping she'd say yes.

"Hmm . . . money's scarce this month. But let Grandma look in her pouch."

Peggy Lomax came out on the porch. "Please, Miss Minnie, can Sandy have a quarter?" she whined.

"A quarter!" Grandma and I both yelled at the same time.

"Well, ma'am," Peggy said, taking a deep breath. She got closer and looked into Grandma's eyes like a cow staring at a new gate. "My mama gits paid today and uh . . . she was gonna give me a quarter for allowance and uh . . . I was gonna split it with Sandy. Only, by the time she gits off work, the store gonna be closed, see? And uh—"

"Well . . . I say," Grandma said, interrupting her. "Sounds like you in kind of a bind." Grandma gave her a sideways glance out of one eye. I studied Peggy's face carefully to see if she'd flinch when she told a lie. But Peggy kept her cool, genteel politeness, as she sat down in the rocker next to my grandmother.

"Well, I guess it ain't nothin' that cain't be fixed." Slowly Grandma opened the silk pouch that she kept pinned to the lace strap inside her bosom. She scattered the meager change she'd saved all month until she found a quarter. "Here you is, child. Y'all promise to be back 'fore dark. You hears me?"

"Yessum! We promise," I screamed as I jumped off the porch.

"And don't spoil yo' appetite for supper! I'll keep it warm."

"I won't!" I yelled again. The moment the quarter touched the palm of my hand, I had stopped listening to anything my grandma said.

Now, I was pretty sure that Peggy's bike was what every girl dreamed about. It was all pink and white with long, candy-cane plastic streamers hanging from the handlebars. A pink-and-white straw basket was in front with Barbie decals pasted on. She had to be the luckiest girl in all of Hooks County. I pumped furiously uphill with Peggy Lomax sitting on the back fin, one hand round my waist, the other holding her skirt down.

"I think it's nice of you to pedal to the store. And I don't mind peddling back. 'Cause ain't that what friends do for each other?" Peggy said.

"Sure, un huh."

"You do wants to be my friend, don't you?"

"Yeah—I guess so," I said, between huffing and puffing.

"You guess so? Really, Sandy Forte. Every girl in Hooks County wants to be my friend. But I chose you to be the first one to ride wit me on my new bike. Ain't that special enough?"

"Well . . . okay, I said we can be friends. But my best and closest friend is my sister, Glory."

"Glory? I don't see her hangin' around anywhere."

"She's at piano practice."

"So that makes us best friends, right?"

56

Illustration by Marlon Hall

"Well sure, maybe. But jus' for today." I hoped that would shut her up, because carrying her uphill and trying to answer all her silly questions was hard work.

Finally, we neared the Johnson Creek Bridge. As we crossed over, I stopped and stared down at the deep, murky water. The undertow had been blamed for drowning a five-year-old boy last summer. He fell in while skimming for catfish. It consisted of mostly swamp weeds, mud, and mosquitoes. All the kids were warned to never go near it without an adult.

"Did you know that the Swamp Thing lives down there?" Peggy said.

"Swamp Thing? No kiddin'!" I was pretty sure she was making it all up.

"I'm not kiddin'! A crazy man named John Earl Jackson went and threw himself in and died. Then his ghost turned into the Swamp Thing. They say it's real ugly and slimy and gots long fingernails that'll claw your eyes out. But it only comes out at night and only messes with people who're by themselves."

"Well, I'm sure glad we's together."

"Me too!" She giggled, holding onto my hand.

Hmmm, I thought. *So, now it's okay to hold my hand? You didn't think so last Easter when we was in front of the whole church. Maybe I oughta snatch my hand away jus' to show you what that feels like.* But I reminded myself that we'd be best friends just for today. So I tossed her sins in the wash bin, as Grandma says and I forgave her.

As we got back on the bike, I pumped even faster until we'd finally crossed the bridge safely. But the more I thought on it, the more I was convinced that maybe there might be some truth to her silly story. I mean, nobody could say what really happened to you when you died. Or even what you might turn into, especially if you weren't buried properly. Uncle Timmy told Grandma that he didn't want to be buried in the old Cedar Springs Cemetery because he said he heard all the coffins floating around under the earth one night after a rainstorm. The next day, it was so soggy that one of the coffins had come up from the ground—open.

When we arrived at the store, I was gob-struck. Before Mr. Parker took over, it was only a feed store with a few supplies and sweets. Now it looked like something out of a fairyland.

Under glass domes were freshly baked goods, apple turnovers, honey buns, fudge brownies, and delicious coconut cream cookies. The glass counter was filled with every penny candy imaginable, including that amazing Laffy Taffy. Mr. Parker, wearing a straw cowboy hat to cover his shiny bald head, sat in his rattan chair, smiling back at us from behind the counter. The more he laughed the more his cherry-red suspenders looked as if they were about to pop under the strain of his huge belly.

"Well, what can I git for you pretty, little ladies?" he asked. "Everything!" I answered, as we anxiously placed our orders.

Later, we sat on the store's steps eating in complete delight. Systematically, I licked the white icing from between each coconut cookie as the crimson sun began to set with quiet dignity.

"I think we oughta' be headin' back. It's nearly dark," I said. Peggy began to giggle. "See that house over yonder?"

"Yeah," I mumbled as I bit into my third piece of taffy.

"Well, my mama's over there workin' for this White lady. And she waitin' on me on account of the White lady's givin' a party and she wants me to help out."

"You sayin' you ain't goin' back with me? But you promised my grandma." I tried to swallow the sticky Laffy Taffy, gulping down hard. I examined her face, making sure I could see her lips move.

"Nope, *you* promised!" she giggled. "Now, I would let you come along wit me, but uggh! . . . you is *so* dirty. Why, you ain't even wearin' no shoes, not to mention . . ." She put her hand up to her nose as if she was trying to hide a bad smell. "*And* don't even ask to ride my bike, 'cause my mama says ain't nobody gonna ride dis bike but me. So I guess y'all better gits to runnin' 'fore it gits dark."

She mounted her pink-and-white bike with the Barbie decals. Her laughter was now out of control. I tried to speak, but the candy had stuck hard in my throat. All I could do was struggle to swallow it down. She put the rest of the candy, bought with my grandmother's money, into her front basket.

"But . . . you just cain't leave me here by myself!"

"Maybe you ought to wait for yo' sister, Glory. Um sure if she be yo' bestest and closest friend lak you claim, she be worried 'bout you. But if not, when y'all crosses dat bridge, watch out fo' the Swamp Thing!" she yelled as she peddled toward the White lady's house.

As I watched her slither across the grassy field, I hardly noticed Mr. Parker closing his store and driving off in his pick-up truck. It dawned on me that I could have asked him for a ride. I tried to stand up under the weight of the words she had just spoken. My legs were refusing to obey me. They just wanted to stay put. Finally, I had to let them know who was making the rules.

Running home that night, the sun long gone, even the owls were silent. "I hope her bike gits stolen," I spoke into the darkness. "No, I *PRAY* it gits stolen and crushed and eaten by a giant bike-eating machine! I even pray that her mama give her the biggest whippin' of her life for eating all that candy 'fore supper!" Then my mind started to settle down and I realized something. I could pray from here to yonder and it wouldn't change the fact that it really wasn't Peggy's fault. It was my fault for thinking that Peggy and I could actually become friends. How eager I had been to throw her sins into the wash bin just because I thought she was pretty and had let me ride her new bike. And to even fool my grandmother into giving part of her savings to someone who could only be described as a deceitful snake.

Blankets of angry clouds began to spread out in the sky hiding the moon's light. So thick was the darkness that I could no longer see my hand in front of my face. No cars passed me on the country road. I felt the warm dirt turn into rough pavement beneath my bare feet as I approached the Johnson Creek Bridge. I took a deep breath and started over.

I tried not to think of John Earl and his ghost or what people looked like when they'd been dead a long time. That creepy-crawly feeling on the back of my neck grew and settled into the pit of my stomach. I became starkly aware of the *gulp-gulp-gulp* of the stagnant water below me. I heard a panting sound. My heart fell to my feet. It was like I was on a rollercoaster with no breaks. The gulping noises got louder and louder and louder. The sound of rusty metal rattling against a chain came towards me, and I slowly stepped back, carefully placing one foot behind the other. As I opened my eyes wider, I thought I saw something emerging from the water. A strange formless creature with glowing green eyes was staring directly at me. Then, like a vapor, it disappeared. But the unrelenting rattling noises continued as I crouched down low, ready to fight. *What was that? Could it be real or imagined?* I shut my eyes because I knew they couldn't be trusted. Suddenly, I heard words that seemed to come from nowhere.

"Be a firefly among devouring locusts and angry wasps. Be a firefly

glowing bright in the darkness! Shine! Light up the hidden works of the enemy!"

Just as I began to grab hold of the courage in those words, the noises started getting even closer and louder—the chains rattling, the creaking of metal rubbing against metal . . . . Then it stopped, and the only sound was the chanting made by my short, quick breaths as I waited, listening.

"Saaaandy, is dat you?" said an oddly familiar voice.

"Leroy! Leroy, is that you?"

"I think so," he said, coming close enough for me to touch his chubby little cheeks. He was riding his brother's rusty, old bike with the chain barely holding everything together.

"Boy, what you doing out here?" I tried to contain my happiness, but it spilled out.

"I dunno. Jus' thought I's come a-lookin' after it gits dark. You kin git on the back, iffin' you want. I'll pedal."

"Did you see anything in the water jus' now?"

"Nope, I cain't see a dag blasted thing. It's nighttime."

We crossed over the bridge, riding on what could hardly be called a bike, and I realized that I was no longer afraid of whatever was lurking in the black waters of Johnson's Creek. I had faced my darkest moment and found a different kind of light. It was the light of knowing. Knowing what a real friend looked like even if you could only touch his chubby cheek.

Last week in Sunday school we were taught about showing mercy and grace to someone who didn't deserve it. That was what I thought I was doing for Peggy Lomax. But instead those things were shown to me by Leroy, because I was the one who really needed it. Not to be undone and with no help from me, my firefly had revealed the spirit of my "good intentions" while exposing my lack of mercy.

As we continued riding down the hill, I shared what was left of my coconut cream cookies with Leroy and he offered me a gift in return. It was the rattler.

"Here, you kin have it if you want."

"Thanks," I said, putting it in my pocket.

"You ain't gotta be scared of nothin', 'cause that's good ol' rattlesnake protection right there!"

"Last night, I cussed out the moon,"I said.

"This mornin', I cussed out the sun," Leroy responded.

"I cussed out the sun, the moon, and all the planets in the sky."

"I cussed out the devil!"

"I cussed out the devil, his wife, and all his nine kids.

"I cussed out God."

"Ooooh! No you didn't."

"Yes I did."

"Shut up! No you didn't."

"You shut up."

"No, you shut up!"

"Last night, I waved at the moon . . ."

We began to laugh like crazy hyenas as the moon came out of the shadows, lighting our pathway home.

CHAPTER 7

BAPTISM

water feels cold, but me don't mind
Preacher goin' too slow, jus' takin' his time
hopin' no snakes movin' down under dar
pushin' me under, kinda makin' me wonder
iffin' I's ever comin' up for air
sho hopin' he don't drown me
keep me jus' lak he found me
hope dat ain't no worms movin' round my feet
I pray de Lord my soul He keep
preacher say now I be washed clean
gots me wondering jus' what he mean
well . . . it wern't so bad I 'spose
'cause jus' lak Jesus did, I rose

It was late summer 1963 and it had been almost two years since Mama has gone back to Chicago. Folks have finally stopped asking me when my mama was coming back to get us, and I've stopped running to the screen door every time a car pulls into our yard. Glory has even stopped writing on account of the letters have all come back stamped "addressee unknown." But for the most part, our lives continued to go on as planned—until the interruption.

Now, this particular interruption started on a Friday night, and it was the first night of the Hooks County Revival. My uncle Ervine Forte was the pastor of the Cedar Grove Baptist Church and was the one who would be leading the revival. That was why Glory and I were preparing especially nice for the occasion. Now, I had been dreading this night since I was first told last month, but there was no discussing the matter. And to add to the horror and dismay, my grandmother was hauling us out in yellow-and-green plaid matching dresses. Dresses that have been donated to us by Mrs. Beatrice V. Sims whose daughter, Velma, died of some rare, but fatal, cough over twenty years ago. Grandma's face was set like stone. She was bound and determined, and no amount of fainting or faking various sicknesses would change her mind. I know because I tried both only a few hours ago.

"Grandma . . . everything is gettin' dark . . . I cain't stand up! Grandma—" I fell to the floor.

"Just don't git that dress dirty or you gonna have to wear dat old one wit the green and purple stripes," she said.

"Grandma . . . I cain't hear nothin'! It's fo' real! Grandma, I'm not kiddin'. I ate some catfish and drank buttermilk. You know both those mixed together kin make you go deaf!"

"Well, I guess you won't hear me when I breaks dat switch off of the tree out yonder."

So before she went outside, I decided to give in and apply Vaseline jelly to my arms, legs, and feet because Grandma said I looked like I'd been kicking flour. Grandma said that I was going to be sitting on the front row, 'cause for me, it was now or never.

You see, after reaching my ninth birthday, I'd been put in the category of what the folks around here call a *heathen* and a *reprobate*. I was told by my uncle Ervine that I was in desperate need of salvation. In fact, the ladies from the Missionary Board of Cedar Grove Baptist Church told me that only the good Lord Himself could set me on the right path. I've stolen, lied, cussed, and had no respect for authority. I'd been accused of chunking rocks at glass windows, ditching school, being prone to picking fights with boys, and relieving myself behind the church steps—all worthy of hellfire.

Was it entirely true? Well, I tried denying most of it, but it seemed they had witnesses. But I believed that everything I did had been for a just and noble cause, none of which could be understood by grown-ups. Now, this truth ain't gonna fall on you like ripe cherries off a tree, as Uncle Zippy says, so let me explain.

For example—I stole peach preserves from the smokehouse because I was hungry. I was hungry because my grandma decided to cook squirrel meat, which I didn't eat on account of I liked little animals and it looked disgusting. And when Grandma asked if I'd taken the peach preserves, I lied because I didn't want to get a whipping. And when I did get a whipping, I cussed because it hurt.

My grandma has tried to tame my behavior by the use of various punishments and rewards such as buying me a Popsicle every time I emptied the slop jars instead of hiding them under the bed. The Missionaries have even tried rubbing my head with annoying—I mean *anointing* oil—but it didn't take. I remember a while back, they tried using that same oil to pray the spinster spirit off Miss Ethel. Then next Sunday morning at church, she'd stood up to give her testimony.

"I thank thee Lord for the Women's Missionary Board, who comes over my house to pray off dat awful spirit of spinsterhood. I 'spect it's too early to claim any good prospects. But I'm mighty hopeful, amen? And next time out, when they gits to laying on hands, I wants dem to cast out dat spirit of irritable bowel syndrome. Why, I'm having an awful time—"

"That'll be enough for right now sister Ethel," admonished Pastor Ervine.

Well, a year had gone by and Miss Ethel still hadn't found a husband. I suspected if she'd got her teeth fixed and a new wig she would have gotten better results.

So as we entered the church, Grandma laid down the ground rules.

"Now Sandy, I wants you to behave yo'self and don't git up, lessin you gotta pee. You understand me?" Grandma held tight to my arm. "And don't look at me in dat tone of voice," she whispered.

"Yes ma'am," I answered solemnly. "But um hungry . . . and um hot and um—"

"Yo' behind 'bout to get a lot hotter, iffin you don't go sit down," she threatened.

Remembering the leather belt she had put in her purse before we left home, I kept quiet and looked for a seat up front next to Glory.

The church was small, hot, and crowded. Ornate tapestries of angels hung on the walls. A huge cross was lit up behind the pulpit. Frowning lady ushers were dressed in white nurses' uniforms, white shoes, and hats. They handed out programs, along with paper fans with a picture of black Jesus holding a baby lamb. The pews were made of pine wood and lined with long, beige cushions. I got into a comfortable position with my elbow resting on the pew's arm.

It is true. I was hungry, hot and tired. Since we wouldn't eat until after the service, I sat there dreaming of fried chicken and apple pie. As I slept peacefully, I was rudely awakened by an usher's long *correcting stick* tapping me hard across the head. I sat back up, still hungry, tired and hot, just to find the service continuing in full swing.

Clarence Tuttle, the choir director, sat at the organ. He was sweating profusely while wearing his lavender and blue pinned-striped-suit with matching bowtie. I wondered why the piano bench didn't collapse under his massive weight and volume. His wife, Bernice, was wearing a matching lavender dress and hat. She was keeping a close eye on Mr. Tuttle as she waited for her cue to begin singing.

It was now time for Pastor Ervine to ask the "unrepentants" to come forward. He started out pleading for us to repent and warned us if we didn't, we'd spend the rest of eternity burning in the fiery pits of hell. This made me begin to wonder if they served fried chicken in hell, it being so hot and all. And how could he be so sure if there was any fire in hell? Had he been to those pits and seen it for himself? Well, I couldn't be sure, but I did know that this persistent begging could prolong the service for at least another hour, which seemed like an eternity.

"Please, is there anyone ready to turn away from their wickedness?" he cried, holding tightly to the pulpit.

I was hoping that someone felt a tiny little bit of repentance, or even remorse, and rose to the occasion, but no one moved. The pastor motioned to the head deacon, who looked all of ninety years old, to place two gold chairs directly facing us in the front row.

Bernice Tuttle began to sing. "He's waiting at the ol' rugged cross! Ohhhh, He's waiting at the ol' rugged cross . . ."

"Y'all don't hear me! Please . . . there has to be—"

As the pastor continued his prolonged pitch for recruits, my stomach reminded me again of its vast emptiness and need for chocolate cake in particular. So, I raised my hand. I was finally . . . well—*overcome*. I guess it was just like a slippery creek. If you gets too close, you're bound to fall in.

As I took a seat, a loud cheer rose up from the congregation. Not to be left out, Glory reluctantly took the other chair next to me. I guess she was just as overcome as I was. The aged but still strong deacon held me firmly down in my seat in case I might have second thoughts.

"Ain't nobody mad but the devil!" the pastor shouted.

One snaggletooth woman in the corner—whom I recognized as Miss Ethel—yelled out, "Amen Pastor! Dat devil sho' is mad!"

So instead of wrapping things up like I'd hoped, they added another unexpected component to the salvation equation—the *inquisition.*

Bending down, Pastor Ervine grabbed hold of both arms of the gold chair and looked deeply into my eyes. "Do you renounce Satan and give your heart to the Lord?" he asked.

"Well . . . yeah, I guess so—"

"Now, you can't guess about this thing, you gotta know!" He was getting closer now and I could clearly see the three moles on the tip of his nose. And his breath smelled a little like pickle juice and some sort of smoke. Maybe he could have actually been in one of those fiery pits and—

"Do you renounce Satan and give your heart to the Lord?" he yelled.

"Well . . . yes, I announce Satan and—"

Loud laughter went throughout the church.

"Listen here, gal," the pastor said, as he straightened his shoulders and stuck out his neck. "Do you *RENOUNCE* Satan and give your heart to the Lord?"

"Yes sir!" I said, sitting up erect in the chair. "I's renounce Satan and give everything to the Lord!"

"Now are you ready to be saved and join the Cedar Grove Baptist Church?"

Fearing the look of mania in his eyes if I messed this thing up again, I answered, "Yes, sir. I's ready!"

A big "Welcome to the family of Christ!" was cried out by the entire church. And with that, I was in. Out of the corner of my eye, I saw the ladies of the Missionary Board standing up fanning and hugging my grandmother as she studied me carefully. Then she gave me the side-eye.

I must admit, I was feeling pretty special. It was like being sworn in to a secret society. Then the pastor mentioned something about a baptism, and I realized this was only the beginning of woes. It seemed part two of the swearing-in ceremony would take place near water, or rather *in* water. He explained that I would have to get *baptized*. And not with just a sprinkle or two of water from a basin—oh no. I would have to be taken down to the river in Red Bank and get dunked. A river loaded with not only catfish, but creepy crawling things that I didn't have names for. But I had not yet become acquainted with this ritual, so I still had a genuine smile on my face as they offered me the right hand of fellowship, welcoming me into the club.

Later that night, I overheard Grandma telling Glory that God had given her a special gift of music, and that she should only sing songs that were holy. *But how can you tell which ones are holy or unholy?* I wondered. Then Grandma said something about Uncle Ervine taking us into town to buy new baptismal clothes. I still didn't fully understand everything, but it all sounded really exciting.

Over the next week, I'd had a chance to think it over and I was kinda liking this baptism thing. It seemed to be working out pretty good for me because here we all were, me, Glory, and Grandma in downtown Texarkana buying new dresses, shoes, and gloves. I wished I had known about baptisms earlier. I wondered if it was possible to get baptized every month. Then I could have twelve new dresses a year! Well, it was worth looking into, I thought.

We started our shopping journey in the children's section of Hampton's department store. The white sales lady brought out two pretty dresses with lace trim around the collar and a big can-can skirt just like Cinderella.

"I like the pink one!" I exclaimed. "Can I try it on, Grandma?"

"I like the purple one," said Glory. "Can I try it on?"

"Well, I guess," Grandma said. "But we need different sizes."

"I'm sorry, ma'am, but the Colored are not allowed to try on the clothes. I'll just measure them and bring out the correct sizes to the counter," the saleslady whispered and quickly walked away.

"Grandma, why does she call us the *Colored*? What does that mean?" I whispered. "And why cain't we try the dresses on? How we gonna know—"

"Hush up! Now she done said the rules and iffin' y'all want a new dress, you gonna have to obey dem rules. Come on heah." She grabbed us both by the hand and went to the register to pay.

Now I didn't understand these *rules* and no one bothered to explain them to me. It was just how things worked. Even when I saw the signs *Colored, Negroes,* or *White Only* over the fountains and bathroom stalls, I just assumed that grown-ups must know something I didn't. Because why would they be so fixated on people's color? There were at least a hundred different colors in my crayon box. What about brown or yellow or pink? I'd seen lots of people that color and they didn't get a special fountain. But after what happened at the store, I vowed to make it my business to find out. Because when Glory and I lived in Chicago, we never saw signs like that. And we could try on anything we wanted. There had to be some kind of difference, but nobody ever talked about it. *I'll ask Uncle Zippy. I bet he can tell me what's going on.*

Later, at Prince's Leather Goods, I tried on a pair of shiny, black patent leather T-strap shoes and admired myself in the mirror. Mr. Prince didn't mind the *Colored* trying them on as long as we put on our new socks first. As Glory walked around looking at shoes, Grandma pulled me close to her. "Do you know why I'm buying y'all these heah new things?" she said.

"Uh . . . 'cause um gittin' baptized?" I hoped this wasn't a trick question.

"Well . . . yes, but that's only part of it," she says.

"Oh, I know why. 'Cause you love me so much," I smiled.

"It's 'cause Jesus loves you so much. And when you goes down in dat water, you His now. Dat makes you a child of God. He's yo' Father, and He gonna take good care of you from now on. You done passed from the old to the new. And these heah new clothes shows you got a brand new life in Jesus Christ. You understand what I jus' said?" I nodded my head yes.

"Dat mean you cain't be doin' like you was before, rippin' and runnin', actin' a fool. God don't like dat. You ain't got me to answer to no more, but now you is got the Lord. You understand me?"

I nodded my head yes again and we took our purchases and left the store.

As Uncle Ervine drove us home, I wondered if Grandma had told this story of being good to Glory. And I also wondered if Glory knew what that meant. I took it to mean that she couldn't be stealing pears from the neighbor's tree no more, or singing unholy songs . . . or blaming me for things that was not my fault. I didn't think our new Father Jesus would like that at all.

So I guess I'm gonna have to be good from now on. Or at least after I gits baptized, I reasoned. I also wondered in my head: *How good is good enough? And who is doin' all the measuring?* Then I heard a voice answer my heart:

"You don't have to be good enough. You are now part of the Eternal, part of the Divine."

CHAPTER 8

I HAD A DREAM

GRANDMA'S FINGER

Dreaming . . .
I was dreaming I could sleep a little more
Warming . . .
getting cold and out of bed was such a chore
Then Grandma's finger, was right up in my face
"It's time to get going. Just look at this place!"
Messy . . .
Should I remove the mess that block the closet door?
Cleaning . . .
Or sweep my room and get stuff off the floor?
I guess . . .
I get distracted and forget things I should do
like when I left my new jacket in the lunchroom at school
Veggies . . .
I can't eat this garbage sitting on my plate
So I stuff it in my pockets and I wait
Too bad . . .
'cause for dessert is my favorite chocolate cake
Then Grandma's finger points, right between my eyes
I get this stern look of anger and God help me if I lie
But then . . .
she puts her arms around me and stays silent for awhile
Grandma's LOVE is the only thing that's bigger than her smile

Grandma didn't have a phone, or even a television for that matter, but I'd never been happier. When something big happened that we needed to see, like Martin Luther King, Jr.'s March on Washington, we watched it at Aunt Hattie's house. Everyone in Hooks who didn't own a TV was there. After King's speech, Grandma said she was glad to live long enough to see such a miracle.

Later, as we all sat on the porch sipping cold, sweet tea, all the kids were quiet and listened to the grown-ups talk about the *I Have a Dream* speech. That was when I learned all about segregation, sit-ins, and my civil rights. I began to understand why they had *Colored* and *White Only* bathrooms and didn't allow us to try on any clothes in Texarkana. I also understood why people in the Southern states like Texas moved *"up North"* to places like Chicago and New York. They wanted the sense that they were just as good as anybody else. They didn't have Jim Crow laws there that made you feel like you didn't belong. Grandma didn't let us go to the movie theater in town because we weren't allowed by law to sit downstairs in the main hall. All the Black people had to enter from the alley and go upstairs to the balcony to watch the movie. She said if our money paid for the same seats as White folks, it shouldn't matter where the seat was located. But even with all the uncivil rights going on, for me it was still better to live in the south with Grandma than anywhere in the north.

In Hooks, we had clean clothes to wear to school every day and a hot breakfast of biscuits, bacon, and eggs from our chickens. And now that Grandma had a "male caller" named Uncle Jack, we had an endless supply of canned peaches and apple preserves. Uncle Jack seemed like our very own Santa Clause, bringing over a burlap bag filled with produce every week. Each time he came over, Grandma's eyes would light up. He'd even come to our school and bring us special treats for lunch.

I'd also learned how to draw water from the well, make

75

quilts from old clothes, and wash sheets and pillowcases until they sparkled white using this product called Liquid Blue. We even made our own soap from lye and perfume. I'd stopped playing hooky from school and started doing my homework. Glory was in the Young People's Choir at church and was starting to laugh and be more sociable. But then Mama showed up and everything changed.

✻ ✻ ✻

Mama's arrival was far more eventful than her departure. She carried with her not only her luggage but also a baby in her belly that would be due in three months. *Was I supposed to welcome this news with joyful anticipation?* I thought of it much like what the state welfare might—another little brown mouth to feed. Grandma said all babies were a gift from God. Well, I wished God would take it back and send us a nice puppy or kitten instead.

Since the two years that she had left, we had received exactly one letter. And that came just before she arrived, asking that someone meet her at the train station. I wondered why she'd come back. Did she miss us? Was it her plan to take us back to Chicago? If it was, she would be in for a surprise.

Mama informed us over gravy and biscuits that she wanted us to come back home with her to Chicago. Feeling like I'd been kicked in the stomach, I ran from the table. I'd rather listen to a donkey bray at midnight than to listen to anything else she had to say. That night, I asked Glory if she wanted to go back, but she never answered me. I hoped her silence wasn't returning.

Two days before we were to leave, I decided to plead my case to Grandma. I found her alone reading her Bible on the front porch.

"Grandma, do you love me and Glory?"

"Now, what kind of silly question is that? Ain't you done felt love from me?"

"Yessum . . . but I ain't been exactly the best kid—like Glory I mean."

"Sandy, what in the world is you aiming at? You know love ain't predicated on how good or bad you is. That's human love and that's selfish. Ain't you understood nothin' 'bout what this here book teaches?" She pointed at the Bible laying on her lap.

"Don't seem like Mama learned nothing from it. Why she ain't even—"

"I ain't gonna sit here and let you berate yo' mama." She closed her Bible and started to get up.

"Listen," I said, holding onto her arm. "If I promise to be the best child ever—even better than Glory—will you let us stay?" "You think this all up to me? I ain't got a bit of say of who goes where and why. Besides, y'all place is wit yo' mama. She's having another baby, and she gonna need y'all to help out 'round the house. The man who got her in the family way done went and gambled up all her money and took off. So you and Glory is all she got."

Sitting back down, Grandma folded her hands over the Bible in her lap and rocked slowly back and forth in her rocking chair. Then she began to hum a song that had been preserved from her ancestors.

As night fell, the house itself seemed to sense my sadness. The doors hinges sighed, and every now and then the floorboards would let out a long, angry cry of despair. But like me, they were only helpless onlookers. I realized that what Grandma had said was true. It really wasn't up to her or me, it was simply the circumstances of life that we'd been born into. And it was right then that I made a decision. If these were the rules I'd have to live by and I couldn't break them, then I wouldn't let them break me. I would bend them instead. And the bending would start tonight. I decided to run away. But where could I go? Who would take me in and hide me until my mother went back to Chicago? Uncle Zippy lived the closest. If I took the shortcut through the Hinman's farm, it would only be a mile and a half. Yes, I could trust good ole Uncle Zippy. But I wasn't so sure about his new wife, Mouse. I'd only met Mouse a few times and she lived up to her name. Her face looked like last year's bird's nest, but Uncle Zippy didn't seem to mind. I thought he loved her because she was so quiet and restrained. When she spoke, which was seldom, she'd squeak a few words while holding her hand over her mouth.

After Glory fell asleep, I found a pillowcase and put in a few items of clothing, five tea cakes from the cupboard, and my toothbrush. Then I headed out the back door.

It wasn't long before I started to rethink this idea of running away at night. As I listened to the sounds of earthly creatures hurrying into their homes, it seemed a much better idea to head out early morning when it was light. Finally, as I emerged from the Hinman's cornfield, I could see the distant light glowing from the window of Uncle Zippy's small cabin. As I approached the back porch, I could make out someone sitting in a rocker going back and forth, back and forth.

"Well, you might as well make yourself known. I'm about to turn in for tonight," Uncle Zippy muttered in his raspy drawl. His thick white mustache, partially brown from dipping snuff, matched his curly white hair and seemed to glisten in the moonlight.

"It's me, Uncle Zippy!" I yelled.

"Well Me, what you doin' out here visiting folks this late?"

I ran up to the porch so he could get a good look at me. "It's Sandy and I'ma runnin' away from home."

"I kin see who you is. But from out yonder, it looks like you was doin' more walking than runnin'. And why you holding yo' belly? You don't feel well?"

"I'm okay. I been tryin' to quiet down my firefly's wings. They keep fluttering around in there. It started when I was out in those cornfields. I guess I was kinda scared of snakes and stuff."

"Well, you had a right to be. You say you got a firefly in yo' belly?"

"Yeah. Grandma gave 'em to me a long time ago when I first went to Chicago. She said it's gonna help if um ever in trouble."

Just then, Mouse's round black eyes peered at me through an opening in the curtains. Her long, gnarled ebony fingers gripped the edges so tight, I was sure she would pull them right off the rods.

"You want somethin' to drink?" Uncle Zippy asked, getting up from the rocker.

"Sure!"

"Maybe we can share a soda pop while we're walking."

"But you ain't fixin' to take me back home yet, is you? I was gonna—"

He ignored me and went inside. Later he emerged with two Cokes.

"Now, did yo' grandma say it was a real firefly?"

"Well . . . she said it was *like* a firefly, but different. It was kinda like a . . . well, it can light up when you's in trouble. Don't you wanna know why I ran away before you starts taking me back home?"

"I betcha it ain't a firefly what's in yo' belly at all. No suh. It's more like what the preacher calls *faith*."

"Faith? Faith's not a something, it's just a word. It's a real firefly all right, 'cause I can feels 'em in my belly and sometimes it lets me know things. I cain't explain it."

"But you just said before that it wern't real."

"No, I mean it's real and it ain't . . . All I know is that Grandma gave 'em to me and it's mine forever," I sighed. "She took her finger and tapped—"

"Nobody can give it to you, 'cause everybody has it. It just got to be activated. You know, turned on. That's what yo' grandma done. She just activated yours."

We started walking through the tall stalks of corn. I was getting a little exasperated talking with Uncle Zippy. Sometimes he made things more complicated than I wanted them to be.

"I don't understand a thing you is talkin' about. Faith? Activate? If all that's true, how would she know how to do that?" I asked.

"Well, I speck she talked to God. He's the one who made faith, and He's the only one that can turn it loose. And seeing how your faith—firefly or whatever you wanna call it—been stirred up, ain't nothing you cain't face that you cain't whip."

"But how's a little firefly gonna whip anything?"

"Baby girl, it ain't the size that's gonna make no never mind. It's the kind of belief you kin put behind it. And the more you believe, the bigger it's gonna git. All things are possible to those who believe."

We walked the rest of the way in silence. I thought it best not to tell him how I'd actually ate and swallowed a live firefly. I also never got around to telling him why I was running away and he never asked. As I tried again to make sense of what he'd said and all of what he didn't say, I realized I would have to save my bending for another day and face whatever the future would bring—as long as I had the help of my firefly.

CHAPTER 9

THE WINTER CLOSET

There's a thick darkness I can feel
It comes in lurking with winter's chill
Can't tell where or when, but still . . .
I know it touched me and it was real
All thru the house I turn on lights
to chase away the winter's night
But in my house is a closet space
neither candle nor lamp lights that place
And when you close the closet door
the darkness creeps around the floor
And then it starts to come alive
Rising up and up 'til it gets inside
And then it starts to make me scream
As my mother wakes me up
it seems—
It was just a silly dream

It was a cold day in late November, even for Chicago. Glory and I had taken the long train ride back north to the big city with Mama. It still hadn't snowed yet, but the frigid, relentless wind blowing off Lake

81

Michigan felt like angry ants biting through my skin. I hugged my book satchel closer to my chest for protection. The only thing that kept me warm, besides the book satchel, was the hot chocolate Ovaltine I'd drunk that morning while watching *Romper Room* on TV. The south-side tenements looked especially dismal and bleak as I passed row upon row of old, worn-down brick buildings. Their gray peeling porches were bare of much-needed paint. Their windows, covered with old newspapers and torn blankets, made desperate attempts to insulate drafty rooms.

I was late, as usual, for school, and my fourth-grade teacher, Mrs. Honeycort, would be waiting with an ugly scowl on her face. Walking the six blocks was easy. My legs were strong. It was my numb fingers that were giving me trouble. The socks I wore over my hands had holes in them. I wasn't able to find the good ones. I couldn't put my hands in my pockets. Had to hold onto the book satchel. Had to keep going. I was running now, the wind howling in my ears. No scarf or hat today, couldn't find them either. The big, blue safety pin that held my coat together was bending under the pressure of my wool jacket. But today was picture day and I had to get there on time.

"Don't be late tomorrow or you won't sit with the class!" Mrs. Honeycort's warning rang in my ears. "And make sure you wear something nice," she'd said as she looked over at me. "Are you listening Sandy Forte?"

"Yes ma'am."

"Speak up!"

"Yes, Mrs. Honeycort."

As the wind beat hard against my face, I silently prayed I wasn't too late. I knew the class had to sit first with hands folded and say—

"Good morning, Mrs. Honeycort." And she would reply, "Good morning, class."

Next, we all had to stand with hands over our hearts for the Pledge of Allegiance and then roll call. *That should take up some time,* I thought.

Rounding the corner, I took off the socks from my hands and shoved them into my pockets. I didn't need any more teasing from the kids in my class today. I'd already had enough of being labeled *Secondhand Sandy* because I only had two dresses to wear, both of which were well known.

One more block to go. There were others who were late. I saw Bobby Richardson and his foster brother Raymond Nettleson were running fast into the school courtyard. I was glad Raymond didn't see me. I'd had enough of his constant teasing. I vowed, if he called me Cootie Patootie one more time, I'd have a go at him. And then I saw Emily Johnson, who was also running with her head down. Her red-checkered scarf was tied tightly over her tiny short braids.

Emily sat behind me in class. She was the only girl that ever really tried to be my friend. She was even poorer than I was. I noticed she wore the same skirt almost every day with a different blouse. I also noticed her penmanship was perfect. It took her almost three weeks to speak to me and ask to borrow a pencil.

Now, I never let anyone borrow my pencils because I only had two and they were nearly down to the nubs. But I knew that she was using a broken black crayon, which made it harder for her to make those beautiful cursive letters. That was why I finally let her borrow one of mine because she was too frightened to ask Miss Honeycort. And when it was time to read out loud, Emily never took her turn. She'd pretend to cough or clear her throat until the teacher would yell, "*Next!*" Sometimes, Mrs. Honeycort would get so angry at her that she'd drag her to "*the Closet*".

The Closet was this small, dark room at the front of the classroom behind Mrs. Honeycort's desk that she reserved for punishment. That's because she wasn't allowed to hit kids anymore with a ruler, or make them stand in front of the class holding up books in each hand. The Closet was, from what I could see, very scary. The light switch was located on the outside wall where she could control it. Whenever the door was opened, I could see a few things like a broom, mop, and bucket. All the kids were deathly afraid of it, which was, of course, exactly what Mrs. Honeycort wanted. She even told us once that there were things in there that might be alive. Which, for any fourth grader, could only mean one thing—the Bogeyman. But, as I recall, Emily was the only one in class who didn't seem to be afraid of the Closet or the Bogeyman. She actually seemed to look forward to it.

When Emily was sentenced to the Closet, Mrs. Honeycort would slam the massive door shut and lock it with her big skeleton key and there would be nothing but silence—not like the whimpering cries we heard when even the bravest of the boys were being punished. Sometimes their sentence would be an hour at a time, but more often, it could last all the way through recess and up until lunchtime.

One time, Raymond got into trouble and was sentenced to the Closet. He yelled and banged so loudly that Mrs. Honeycort had to use the ruler on him, even though it was forbidden. It was all the kids could talk about at recess. Someone suggested that maybe Raymond had been yelling because the Bogeyman was blowing on the back of his neck. I never understood why the Bogeyman would simply want to blow on your neck. I didn't know anything about Bogeymen, but I did know something about being hungry and my suspicions were that the Bogeyman was hungry and just wanted a little taste of Raymond. I also knew that I would never ever allow myself to be put inside the Closet.

I got inside just as the second tardy bell rang. As I ran up the stairs, out of breath, I could see Mrs. Honeycort standing in front of room 4B. Her eyes were narrowed into small slits and her tight, thin mouth was definitely not smiling. She was holding a long wooden ruler, patting it against her skinny black skirt. Then she pulled her gray sweater closer together, as if to fight off a chill in the air. All the kids were already lined up according to height alongside the wall in the classroom.

"Well . . . I see you managed to come to school today. Late as usual," she snapped. She tapped the pointer inside the palm of her hand. "What did I tell you yesterday, young lady?"

Trying to catch my breath, I stammered, "You said . . . you said . . . you said—"

"Hurry, go inside and take off that coat and get in line."

"Yes ma'am!"

"And you have exactly thirty seconds! One, two, three, four . . ."

As I ran past the kids to the cloakroom, I could hear them all snickering at me. But my, how nice they all looked. The girls were wearing their best dresses with matching ribbons in their freshly pressed hair. All the boys were sporting white shirts with ties and sharply creased black pants. Their shoes were polished and shined. Even Emily, who had rushed past me, had on what looked like a new yellow dress with a white ribbon tied in a bow around her head. I had tried to comb my hair this morning the best I could, but it was short and needed pressing. I couldn't braid worth a darn and Mama was *"busy"*, so I'd found a shoelace and made a ponytail. I was sure the wind had pretty much destroyed what little I had done.

Even though I had bragged to the other girls that I was going to have a new dress for picture day, I still had on what I'd worn the last two days in a row. Mama hadn't had time to do the laundry, which she usually did once a month. And since she'd just had a new baby girl named Lola, she couldn't go back to work. We now relied on the Illinois state government for welfare money and a food stamp voucher for groceries every month.

"What's taking you so long?" Mrs. Honeycort now stood in the doorway looking down at me.

"I—I cain't git the pin out," I lied as I fumbled with the big safety pin that held my coat together.

"Well, let me see . . ." She put the pointer down on the floor and grabbed hold of the pin.

"No!" I yelled, jerking away. "I kin do it."

Miss Honeycort grabbed the pin again. "Let me—"

"No! I kin do it!"

Finally, she let go and I pretended to try to open it again, turning away so she couldn't see that I was only pretending. I couldn't open my coat. I *wouldn't* open my coat and let her and all the kids see my shame. The shame of the same dirty, brown cotton dress with the collar still torn and two buttons in the back still missing, that I'd worn all year to school. I didn't know much about what I should look like in fourth grade, but I knew what I *shouldn't* look like.

And today, for the first time in my life, I knew what being ashamed felt like. I had never thought of myself as poor—needy, maybe. There had been things I'd wanted for Christmas that I'd seen other kids my age have. Like when I was five and saw the girl next door with a hula hoop, I could have cried. And I did, every time I listened to the radio when Alvin and the Chipmunks would sing, *"—and I still want my hoola hoop—"* in the "Chipmunk Song".

But now I didn't feel like I was the same as everyone else. I felt different and I didn't like it. No, I couldn't take my coat off—I would never take my coat off. I didn't want to look into Mrs. Honeycort's eyes and see a look of pity and disgust staring back at me. I didn't want to look down at myself and feel the same.

Mrs. Honeycort swung me around, strong and hard. "Listen here, young lady. You must unfasten that coat now," she said through gritted teeth. "You will not make us late because the photographer won't like it. Understood? Now if you won't let me unfasten that thing, you can just stay here."

I looked towards the doorway, unsure if I should try to make a run for it. I wanted desperately to be in the picture with the class, but how could I let them see my dress? They would now know what I knew, that I was one of those *"poor unfortunates"*— Those people who begged on street corners, who got their clothes from church donation bins, or waited at back doors of bakeries for the stale bread and pastries they would throw away, or asked for credit from the grocery store owners after closing. Sadly, I was now an official member.

"Cain't I jus' leave my coat on?" I pleaded.

It seemed that was all Mrs. Honeycort could take. She grabbed me by the arm and began leading me towards the Closet. As she pushed me forward, I locked onto her legs with my hands, holding on with all the strength of someone being led to the gas chamber.

"Let me go, you little—"

She struggled furiously, trying to unlock me, but my tiny, strong fingers held firm, gripping her nylon stockings until I could feel them begin to snag.

"You're tearing my nylons!" she screamed.

By now, we were like performers in a mad ballet, dancing around and around in front of the closet door. She tumbled onto the floor, tripping over my legs as they wrapped around her. The kids had gotten out of formation against the wall and were standing in the doorway of the Closet. Mrs. Honeycort had managed to drag both of us inside as they all yelled, "Fight, fight, fight!"

"Raymond! Go get the principal!" she screamed.

Raymond darted away like a hungry mosquito down the hallway to the principal's office.

As we continued to wrestle inside the Closet, I was determined that she would not win this battle. I fought with the vigor of a world lightweight champion. I held onto her hair, her sweater, her earring—anything so she couldn't get away.

Finally, the Principal Mrs. Hewlett arrived. She shifted her gaze from me to Mrs. Honeycort. "What the—Mrs. Honeycort! Get up off that floor!"

"Get this beast off me!" Mrs. Honeycort screamed.

Mrs. Hewlett came into the Closet and seized hold of my ponytail, pulling hard, bringing me back to reality. All the kids were standing outside the Closet looking on in awe. Mrs. Hewlett lifted me up as if she was removing a puppy from its mother.

I quickly turned around and bit her hard on the hand, forcing her to release me. She screamed, running out holding her hand. Suddenly, I saw a flicker of light. It was my firefly illuminating the dreaded skeleton key that was lying on the floor. I picked it up and bolted out, locking the door with Mrs. Honeycort inside.

Running out the classroom, down the hall, I suddenly heard someone running behind me. I turned around and saw that it was Emily.

"Wait!" she yelled. Breathing hard, I skidded to a halt. She tied her red-checkered scarf around my head and scampered back to the classroom.

As I ran through the empty courtyard, I could still hear Mrs. Honeycort screaming and banging on the door inside the closet. I thought she sounded like what a real Bogeyman would sound like, if you had him trapped. I kept running through the playground and out the gates of the chain-link fence.

The cold air hit my face like an invisible icy mist, making me gasp and feel invigorated. I reached inside my pocket for my socks but felt the skeleton key instead. My socks must have fallen out and lay somewhere in the darkness of the Closet.

I heard the window of the third-floor classroom as it flung open. Turning around, I saw Mrs. Hewlett's face peering down as I listened to the faint cries of Mrs. Honeycort. "Don't come back without your mother!" Mrs. Hewlett yelled.

"I won't!" I yelled back as I ran down the street.

As I crossed the street from my school, the first snowflakes of winter began to fall. They felt like big, wet kisses on my face. Suddenly, it started to come down, harder and faster, almost obscuring my view of the sidewalk. I ran faster, fighting against snow and wind. Then, my mind did a spinning rewind and I was four years old again at my grandmother's house on Christmas Eve. Aunt Sarah had gone into the back woods with an ax and cut down a huge spruce tree. I had begged to go with her, but she'd taken Glory instead. When they returned, they both had such looks of triumph on their faces as they dragged the tree into the living room. My grandmother frowned when she noticed the floor was covered with mud, pine needles, and silver bugs that was also part of their forest offering.

The next morning was Christmas, and both Glory and I were up at dawn, but not before Grandma. She was already at the kitchen stove preparing our breakfast of grits, fried eggs, and cheese toast with a big jar of homemade peach preserves.

"Grandma, where's our presents?" I said, pulling at her dress.

"You mean yo' dolls? Y'all gotta wait 'til after supper tonight so you kin be surprised."

"But how we gonna be surprised?" Glory said. "We don' already seen you make 'em last night on the sewing machine."

"Well, it don't make no never mind. Gifts ought to be given out proper, so um gonna wrap 'em up in newspaper first. All the kin folks be comin' over tonight and they gonna want to watch you open your gifts and share in the happiness too so—"

"But, Grandma, what about *your* happiness? We ain't got no present for you. What you gonna open after supper?"

"What you talkin' 'bout, lil' girl? I done got two gifts already, and dat's more than you both."

"Who gave you a present? Was it Aunt Sarah?" Glory asked.

"Well suh, one was given to me by God. And dat's the gift of the Holy Spirit. The other present was sent a long time ago by your mama. And dat be you two. Now go eat your breakfast fo' it gits cold."

As my Christmas memories slowly faded, I returned back to my present reality. Running up the crumbling concrete stairs, I made a silent wish that my grandmother would greet me at the door, but no one was there. Instead when I entered, I saw Mama at the kitchen table making something. It looked like a chocolate cake! Was it somebody's birthday?

"Mama, what's going on?" I said excitedly.

"Is you done forgot? Tomorrow's Thanksgiving and yo' uncle Pete, his new wife, and all they kids are coming over here for dinner. I'm making a turkey, dressing, and sweet potato pie too, so git out of my kitchen. And next week, we gonna be movin' across town so . . ."

"But Mama, somethin' happened today at school and they said—"

"I said git out of my kitchen! Caint you see um busy?"

Well, I guess the news of the Closet would have to wait. At least until after Thanksgiving. Now I would concentrate on the wonderful news I had just been given. I would be having a Thanksgiving dinner with my family, just like all the other people in my neighborhood. Slowly, the shame I had felt because of my clothes was being replaced with a sense of hopefulness. If things could change so fast from having nothing to having a big turkey with all the trimmings, then anything was possible.

I was glad that tomorrow was Thanksgiving because now I realized I had so much to be thankful for. Even though I didn't have a fancy new dress for picture day, at least I had a dress. And when we went to the laundry, I'd have two more. And even though I didn't get a chance to take my school picture, I had gotten a chance to take away the key to the Closet, and neither

I, nor anyone else, would ever get locked inside again. And I also found out that I had a real friend named Emily who cared about me being cold. Yes, I had a lot to be thankful for. All I had to do was look around. Coming home and seeing Mama cooking in the kitchen, knowing we would all be together for Thanksgiving, made up for every bad thing that had happened. At least for now the cloud of shame had lifted and my light of hope shone even brighter than before. My firefly had made sure of that. I knew he must have given me the strength to fight off Mrs. Honeycort and find the key. I couldn't honestly be sure if Heaven and Earth had forever shifted in my favor, but I had surely learned how to bend and not break.

CHAPTER 10

THE GIFT OF FAITH

now faith is a substance
dat's what I been told
wern't nothing you could see
but somethin' you could hold
thinkin' it was a mustard seed,
I sealed it in a box
but when I went to take it out
no key would fit the lock
the only key was in my heart
made of light to destroy the dark
whatever the need, great or small
dat little seed can fix it all
jus' keep on believing' and never doubt
'cause God said He'd work it out
dis one thing I learned for sure
dat faith is real, faith is pure
either you got it, or you don't
if you cain't believe it, then you won't
when things happen, don't ask why
jus' find dat seed and you'll get by

Winter's frozen landscape had disappeared in Chicago and so had the optimism of spring and games of summer. It was now September 1964 and school had finally started. I was glad we'd moved to a new school district. I had changed a total of four different schools since being in Mrs. Honeycort's class. I prayed I'd never have to see Beaumont Elementary again. I heard it took quite a while before the janitor came and freed Mrs. Honeycort from the closet. Let's hope when she *"came out"* she was a new person.

I was the tallest girl in my fifth grade class. And it seemed like I grew out of my clothes every few weeks. I had even grown three inches taller than Glory. We both cut our bangs so we could look like The Beatles. They were a new pop group from England that had just come to America. But no matter what I did to fit in, I still felt clumsy and awkward, and all the boys said I had the *"cooties"*. Every day some random kids would chase me home after school throwing rocks and saying bad things about my mother. Why, they knew nothing about her. My mother was beautiful, she made sure of that. Even though she didn't make much money at her job as a waitress in Walgreens, her closet was filled with pretty dresses, fur coats and fancy shoes. She said if something was ripped or stained, the shop owners sold it for half price. And when she wore her cat-eye sunglasses with her long, fake ponytail, she looked just like someone in a Glamour magazine. No, they knew nothing about my mother.

The next month they raised our rent so my mother decided to move again to a cheaper, more rundown apartment in a different neighborhood. It gave me the opportunity to transfer to yet another new school. Now I had a chance to make friends and maybe, just maybe, I might even be popular! I imagined that pretty girls would invite me over for sleepovers and birthday parties, and we would braid each other's hair and play double-dutch and boys would think I was cute and pass me notes in class and . . . *Yes, only good things will happen to me here,* I vowed. I remembered my Grandma saying, *"Show yo'self friendly and friends will show up"*. I took comfort in those simple words.

* * *

On the first day at George Washington Middle School, I was told to stand up and was introduced as the new kid by my teacher Mr. Bennett. He was tall and broad shouldered. He wore a nice blue suit, white shirt and matching blue tie. He had a thin mustache, and his wavy black hair was slicked back, which made him look like a movie star. He was by far the handsomest man I'd ever seen in person. I was pretty sure that my secret adoration of him was shared by half the female teachers in the school. They'd stop by throughout the day, one by one. Some would come in and whisper little things in his ear, while others would look eagerly through the glass window in the door and beckon him out to the hallway. He was always very polite, but I could tell he was getting annoyed.

One Monday, at the end of the day, Mr. Bennett announced to the class that we were going to the Museum of Science and Industry on Friday and that it would cost us each $1.25. We'd also have to bring a sack lunch. He said that we would be representing our school, and that we should be dressed properly—meaning no unkempt hair and no dirty sneakers. Boys should have on white shirts and dark slacks only. Victoria, who sat in front of me, was chosen to pass out the permission slips. I raised my hand, but she skipped my desk. I sensed it was something about me that she didn't like.

But Victoria was perfect. In comparison, she was even more perfect than Peggy Lomax. Her "Beatle cut" shiny bangs were trimmed just above her thick, black eyebrows. She wore a well-starched and ironed yellow dress that matched her socks. And when she walked, she had a graceful little bounce in her step. As I watched her I thought, some people were just born under a lucky star. They never had to want or wish for anything, it just came to them naturally. I was sure she could have any friend she wanted.

Mr. Bennett personally gave me my permission slip. And when he bent down close to me, I got a small whiff of his rich cologne. Its masculine, woodsy fragrance smelled of green pastures, Old Spice, and leather all mixed together. I sat there motionless, wondering if he could hear the pounding of my heart. Finally, he just put the slip of paper on my desk and walked back to the front of the class.

Walking home after school, I tried to formulate a plan that would come up with a sack lunch, new shoes, and the money I needed for the trip. I knew I would have to get everything myself because I had learned that asking Mama for anything was useless. She'd always have some sort of excuse.

"Mama, can we go out and have hamburgers tonight?" I'd ask.

"You got some fast food money? It's some leftover beans in that pot."

"But Mama, we've had beans every day for three weeks. We tired of beans."

"Well you ain't really hungry then, are you?"

"Mama, can Glory and me go to the movies to see—"

"What? Do I look like I'm made out of money?"

"Mama, I need some new—"

"You *need*? What you need is a job. Ain't you old enough to start babysitting?"

Money, money, money . . . where could I get my hands on it? I thought about how Glory and I had made money one summer selling Kool-Aid for a nickel a cup. But it was too cold outside now, and I didn't have money to buy paper cups. Then it dawned on me. Soda pop bottles! That was it! If I returned one to the store, I could get two cents for every glass bottle and fifteen cents for every milk bottle. I remembered when Glory and I wanted to see the latest Elvis movie that came out, we'd gone from door to door asking for people's empty soda pop bottles. We'd hustle until we had returned enough bottles for two tickets and one box of popcorn. So if I started looking tonight when I got home, I could make a dollar or even more by Friday. Now the hard part: shoes and a sack lunch. I didn't own any nice shoes like those shiny, black patent leather ones the girls wore when they wanted to dress up. I only had the ones my grandmother had bought me two years ago and were much too small now.

Sometimes at night while lying in bed, I'd think about how much I missed Hooks and being with my grandmother. I remembered how she'd take us with her, when she visited the sick and shut-ins at their houses. And Uncle Jack would take us into town and buy us nice new shoes. Living with Grandma was the hope I held onto and the memories I guarded.

I looked down and inspected my three-dollar gym shoes, the only ones I owned. They were totally worn out. Cheap and flimsy, they would only be good for another month. Then they would start to come apart until the rubber around the edges would separate from the shoe and my big toe would stick out front. And if it rained, or if I stepped into a puddle, I would be in big trouble. Then every time I walked, my shoe would flap open making a clapping noise. My shoes were now very close to the *clapping* stage. The one thing I found that helped bind them together for a while was Elmer's glue.

Well, on to a sack lunch. *Hmmm . . .* Unless it was a holiday we usually ate beans and neck bones with hot water cornbread every night. I was pretty sure the kids would laugh me off the bus if they saw me eating a neck bone and cornbread sandwich for lunch. No, I wasn't ready for that level of torture.

When I reached my apartment, what did I see?—Three empty Pepsi Cola bottles just sitting on the stoop. I couldn't believe my luck. I ran upstairs to find a shopping bag to put them in.

I noticed Mama was asleep on the sofa. Now that God had *gifted* her with another baby, she wasn't allowed to work at her job as a waitress anymore, because she had to stand for long hours. Desperate, she'd let her boyfriend, Charlie Cole, and his two kids move in to help with the rent. The bonus was that Mama could get more money from the state welfare agency for the amount of children she had. With Charlie Cole's two kids—one four-year-old boy named Larry, who we called Bubba, and five-year-old Mary—she could claim a total of five kids.

Charlie Cole was a gambler and would usually lose most of his paycheck from the tire factory playing cards, way before he reached home on paydays. But when he did manage to keep a few dollars, he taught Glory and me the fine art of playing dice and winning at cards. First, he'd give us an allowance of twenty-five cents. Then, he'd tell us we could double it, if we played a card game of *Pitty-Pat* with him. When he taught us the game, it seemed simple enough, but after three hands we'd lose, and just like that our quarters were back in his pocket. And he taught me one more thing—the only way to win was not to play.

Glory was outside in the alley playing jump rope with her new friends. And my other three siblings were sitting on the floor watching cartoons. I grabbed an empty shopping bag and ran back downstairs.

I walked and walked, block after block, searching for bottles. I looked through alleyways and under viaducts until my bag was finally full. It was nearly dark when I carefully made my way to the grocery store for my deposit money. But the devil never sleeps. He kept his agents on the prowl in the form of Raymond Nettleson from my old school, Beaumont Elementary. Raymond spotted me from across the street. He ran over and stood in front of me, blocking my way. Then he began to taunt me. His dry, crusty lips formed into a snarl.

"Yo' mama don't wear no draws . . . I saw her when she took 'em off—She hung 'em on the wall—dem bugs refuse to crawl—hahahaha!"

I peered over my bag to see his dirty face. His eyes looked at me menacingly. I pushed past him and continued on my mission.

"PBH, PBH! Professional Bottle Hustler!" he cackled. "Hey, PBH, you got a license to carry all dem bottles?"

I ignored him. Everyone in the neighborhood knew his story. He was one of the true "*poor unfortunates*". A kid who'd been passed around to different foster homes when the families got tired of him. He always looked like an angry, unwanted pet, which kind of made me feel sorry for him because I knew what it felt like to be unwanted. But sometimes he liked to take his anger out on others.

I kept walking to the store. It was only another half block. He moved behind me and continued his mocking song.

"Yo' mama don't wear no draws—I saw her when she took 'em off—She laid 'em in the street—dem cars went beep-beep-beep! Hahahaha!" he squealed, bending over with laughter.

"Well, at least I got a mama!" I shouted back.

Perhaps that wasn't the most tactful thing I could have said. He made a running dash towards me and pushed me to the ground. My bottles went helter-skelter into the street. Every one of them broken.

"That's what you git! You don't know a dang-blasted thing 'bout my mama! And you ain't even got no daddy, 'cause he done left yo' mama a long time ago!" he yelled, and ran down the street. I laid there motionless, staring at my broken dreams glistening under the streetlamp. All hopes of going on the field trip lay in a heap of glass on the sidewalk. What right did I have to try and be anything other than what I was—a ghetto Black kid living on the third floor of a run down apartment building. I had nothing—no money, no decent shoes, and no lunch. Try as I might, I couldn't fool myself—I, too, was one of the *"poor unfortunates"*—a PBH with no real father, just like Raymond had said. I wasn't even mad at him for pushing me down. I figured I shouldn't have said that about me having a mother and he didn't. But that didn't erase the fact that there was no way I would be going on the field trip with my class.

The next few days were wretched. At night, I continued to have a great time feeling sorry for myself as I lay on my cot in the living room. Then, like a flash, the firefly began to light up my imagination, and it was summer again. I was with Grandma at Hampton's department store just before I got baptized. My grandmother's words came rushing back to me as faith washed away fear.

"Now you gonna git baptized. And when you goes down in dat water, you belong to Jesus now. Dat make you a child of God and He gonna take care of you from now on. He gonna provide for you. Iffin you need anything, you kin go to Him, 'cause He's yo' father now."

Was this really true? One thing I knew for sure was true and that was my grandmother had never lied to me. I remembered when she prayed for the firefly to be stirred up inside me and how the misty fog came in and covered her face. I remembered what I felt like afterwards. Maybe this same God who had answered her prayers would answer mine. So with that, I closed my eyes, put my hands together, and prayed.

"Dear Jesus . . . Hello. . . uh . . . now I lay me down to sleep. I pray the Lord my soul to keep. I . . . I . . . Listen, my grandma says I'm yours now, since I was baptized and that you is my daddy. So, Daddy, I need one dollar and twenty-five cents to go on the museum trip tomorrow, and I also need a pair of black patent leather shoes and a sack lunch. Thanks . . . I mean, amen. Oh yeah, and, Daddy, please give Raymond a real mama. Amen."

Early the next morning, I woke up just as dawn was breaking. Everyone else was still asleep. Charlie Cole was snoring loudly underneath a blanket on the love seat. Mama was laid out on the couch. The others were sleeping on various rollaway beds in our one-bedroom apartment. And there stood a huge cardboard box in the middle of the living room. I inched towards it, not sure what to expect.

Inside I found shoes. All kinds of shoes in all sizes and colors. I pulled them out the box. They still had the tags on them, so they were brand new. T-strap patent leather, brown suede, black-and-white oxfords, penny loafers . . . —it seemed endless. I screamed at the top of my lungs. My mother sat up, not fully awake. Glory and Bubba woke up and ran over to the box.

"Mama, Mama! Look! New shoes, we got new shoes!" I screamed again.

"Girl, stop screaming, it ain't even daylight!" Mama said.

"But where dey all come from?" I said, lowering my voice.

"Well . . . Charlie Cole, dat ol' bald-headed peach, he won dem shoes last night in a crap game. Him and dis here man was gambling and the man ran out of money, so he had a bunch of shoes in his trunk and he gambled for the whole box and lost. So, here dey is."

With that, she put the cover over her head and went back to sleep. To add to the confusion, someone was knocking on the back door. Bubba followed Glory as she went over and opened it. It was Raymond Lee Nettleson standing next to a very large, very ebony-colored woman. She had a huge bosom and was wearing a green-flowered dress and matching hat. She seemed out of breath from walking up our three flights of stairs.

"Is Sandy Forte livin' here?" asked the woman.

"Yes, ma'am, there she is," Glory said, pointing at me.

I was so busy trying on shoes, I hardly looked up.

"Sandy, git over here! You in trouble again," Bubba yelled.

"She ain't in no trouble. Raymond's got something for her," the woman said, clutching her big, velvet-green pocketbook. Curious now, I went to the door.

"I'm Annie Pearl Bradshaw, Raymond's foster mother. Raymond's got something he wants to give you." Raymond held out his balled-up fist.

"Go on, open yo' hand, boy. Give it to her!" Mrs. Bradshaw said.

Raymond dropped six quarters into my hand. I was confused. "What's this for?" I asked.

"Well, I hears Raymond bragging to his foster brothers the other day 'bout how he knocked you down and made you break all the bottles you was fixin' to deposit at the store. And I needs to teach him you don't do ugly, or ugly will come back to you. So he's giving you his weekly allowance to make up for it. Now say you sorry, Raymond."

"I's sorry," he said, hanging his head.

At that moment, I actually had to fight the impulse to kiss him. One dollar and fifty cents! Twenty-five cents more than I needed. I stared at the coins as though they were about to vanish any second. When they'd finally left, I ran to find the permission slip, put on a clean dress, and a brand new pair of black patent leather, T-strap shoes. Then I hurried off.

As I neared the school, it dawned on me that I didn't have a sack lunch. *What would everybody think when they started to eat and I sat there with nothing?* Finally, I stopped just across the street from the school. The crossing guard lady was trying to usher me across, but I couldn't move. I stood there as big, salty tears streamed down my face. There was nothing I could do, nowhere I could go.

The crossing guard lady came over to me. "Honey,—what's wrong?" She bent down to put her hand on my shoulder.

"I-I . . ."

"Honey, you better get to school or you gonna be late."

"I-I can't . . . I ain't got no lunch and we going on a trip . . . —and everybody gonna laugh at me . . ."

With that, the lady grabbed me by the hand and we rushed across the street where the basement grocery store was. We went straight to the meat counter.

"Dean, get this child any kind of sandwich she wants," she said.

"What you want, sweetheart? I got cheese, bologna, sliced ham, salami . . . —" Dean bragged as he pointed out his deli collection.

"Cheese and ham?" I asked, hoping that wasn't costing too much.

"How 'bout some salami too just for the heck of it?" Dean asked, smiling.

"Sure, why not?" she said, hugging my shoulders.

I stood there, fluctuating somewhere between joy, amazement, and disbelief. It seemed I had turned into Cinderella and she was my fairy godmother. Next, the lady bought me potato chips, cookies, and a large apple juice. After she paid, she gave me the bag. "Now you hurry up to school before that bus leaves."

"Thank you, Ma'am. My mama will pay you back when—"

"Don't you worry about that. This was on me. Now get!" She pushed me towards the school.

I got there just in time as they were boarding the bus. I gave Mr. Bennett the permission slip and the money. Then I took a seat by the window.

"Why don't you sit next to me?" Victoria said across the aisle. Was I really hearing her correctly? Not waiting for a second invitation, I moved over and we compared lunch sacks. Mine was twice as big as hers.

Stepping down off the bus in front of the museum, I glanced up at the reflective mirror hanging near the exit. There I was, in a brand new pair of shoes, with a huge sack lunch, getting ready to go to the Museum of Science and Industry in Hyde Park. There was no doubt in my mind that some kind of miracle had occurred. How could I have ever imagined what I saw in the mirror before me? The firefly's wings began to flutter, creating a tingling sensation that welled up inside me. That's when I had to forcefully stop the tears from flowing. Now I was sure of one thing: I would never think of myself as a *"poor unfortunate"* again. How could I? This was what my grandmother had tried to teach me, but I had to learn it myself. It was all about faith, like Uncle Zippy said, not fortune. I was also sure of one more thing—I wouldn't ever have to imagine some faceless, nameless man stranded on an island as my father. I did have a real father and He owned everything. His name was Jesus, and He was only a prayer away. I smiled, turning my face upward into the warmth of my Father's hand.

CHAPTER 11

GORILLA GIRL

if I was to climb a jungle tree
wonder what strange beast I might see
cain't say none would look like me . . .
I think I stays here on the ground
where familiar things is all around.
it grinned down at me, but still . . .
might try to maim, or even kill
don't knows what that thing might do
guess I stays down here wit you
'cause it wasn't what, but it was who

Sometimes in our lives we've encountered people who were not so nice to us. Not everyone we meet may want to be our friends. And we might not want to be their friend either. But as my grandma always said, "Some of the lessons you learn ain't always in a schoolbook. And they be the hardest ones of all." The one I learned was very simple. It didn't cost you anything to give out kindness and understanding, but meanness could make you the poorest person in the world.

I was 11 years old and had only been at Wrigley Middle School for three weeks, but I had noticed a particularly vicious girl who had a fondness for torture. She was even bigger and taller than most of the other left-behinds and had an uncanny resemblance to a wild gorilla. With great ape-like hands, she would grab food from the trays of timid, smaller kids in the cafeteria at lunchtime. Her reign of terror was random, based purely on animal instincts. No one ever knew who her next victim might be.

The street code of conduct used to dictate that if anybody wanted to pick a fight with you, they'd usually wait until after school. They'd go through the ritual of menacing you all day in class with hand gestures, like putting both fists up to their eyes and nose and pointing to the clock. This signified what they were going to do to you when the bell rang at three-fifteen. But nooo, not this girl. She'd fight you right inside school, no matter where, no matter what time it was. Her real name was Amanda Lewis, but everyone secretly called her Gorilla Girl.

Now, the only time I'd ever eaten anything close to the foods I'd seen advertised on television was at lunchtime in the school cafeteria. I felt grateful and blessed to give the lunch lady my blue government-issued get-lunch-for-free-cause-you're-a-poor-kid card and purchase my hamburger, fries, and chocolate milk with dessert. Some kids were embarrassed to show their blue card, but not me. When it came to free, real food, I had no shame.

One day, Gorilla Girl's predatory instincts caused her to focus her beady eyes on me and my lunch tray. Her gaze sent chills through me and I started to panic. Here was this thick, no-neck monster eyeballing me—thinking about taking away the one thing that made it worth getting up and going to school. I went into fight mode because I didn't think I could just give up my cherished meal, even to the great ape. As I watched her huge body lumber over to my table, I steeled myself for the inevitable.

"Gimme," she said as she tried to snatch my hamburger off the plate. Bravely, I grabbed her massive hand, pinching it as hard as I could.

"Is you trying to hurt me?" she asked with a puzzled look on her face.

"Uh . . . no. I'm encouraging you to move away and leave my hamburger alone."

She removed my hand from hers, grabbed hold of my hamburger, shoved it into her mouth, and drank down the rest of my chocolate milk.

Why wasn't her own lunch enough? What desperate poverty, or hunger, drove her to deprive others of their food? It was anyone's guess. But trying to gain some understanding of what made her do what she did never entered my head. All I could think was, *This Gorilla Girl just ate my food.* No one told the teachers because everyone was deathly afraid of her and her family tribe of apes living at home. Even the Principal Mr. Blackwell was known to back away when she came down the hall. I admit, instead of fight mode I resorted to flight mode and went hungry that day. But I vowed that it would be the last time she'd take anyone's meal again. I would put a stop to her once and for all.

That night, while eating my plate of beans in front of the television, an advertisement came on about a strong laxative called *All B Gone.* It guaranteed results within twenty-four hours or your money back. It was the strongest available without a doctor's prescription. Grandma always said, "What you allow is what's gonna continue." So with that in mind, I paid a visit to the corner drugstore.

The next morning before school, I staked out the shelf where All B Gone was located. And there it was—a huge bottle filled with this thick, black syrup. The warning label on the back read, "*To be used with caution. For adults only! Take one teaspoon once a day, only!— Any more could possibly prove fatal.*"

"But would it work for or has it been tested on primates?" I said to no one in particular. In any case, it was worth a try. I looked around. I knew the store detective would be monitoring the kids near the candy aisle, so when I saw my chance, I took it. I grabbed the bottle and put it in my book satchel.

The next day, as I got my usual hamburger and chocolate milk, both excitement and terror gripped me. I took a deep breath to steady my shaking hands and put my tray down on the table next to the wastebasket. I opened the bottle of All B Gone. *What if she taste the milk and sees there's something wrong? What if she squeezes me with her big, huge hands and—*

As I opened the carton of chocolate milk, some of it spilled onto the table. I quickly poured out two-thirds of the contents into the wastebasket. Next, I poured as much of the All B Gone into the carton as I could. I shook up the mixture and threw the bottle into the trash. I made my way to my usual spot by the windows and waited. I didn't have to wait long.

There she was, grabbing a fistful of fries from one scared little kid's plate. This was in full view of the unlucky girl chosen to fill the shoes of the lunch monitor that day. Gorilla Girl was on her way to my side of the room when the uninitiated lunch monitor decided to be brave and came over to stop her. The monitor stood in front of Gorilla Girl with her palms open wide in the *"halt"* position. I cringed, fearing for the lunch monitor's life, as well as thinking that all my plans would be destroyed. But as I suspected, Gorilla Girl ran true to form; she picked up the lunch monitor and flung her to the ground.

"Kill you," was all she uttered as she continued on her way, lurching towards me.

Creature of habit that she was, she grabbed my hamburger, shoving it down in two gulps, and finished it off with the chocolate milk. She never even paused to wonder about the change of flavor.

The next day at lunch, there was a surprising calm in the air. There were no signs of Gorilla Girl anywhere—not that day, nor the next, nor the next. It was like Christmas Eve, the Fourth of July, and Easter Sunday all rolled into one, because just like that, with no explanation, she was gone. By Friday, the school was all abuzz over what had happened to Gorilla Girl. Seemed the poor beast had been rushed by ambulance to the hospital after being found on the floor of the girls' restroom, suffering from what could only be described as a *cute intestinal inflammation*. Rumor said she had been found lying in a horrifying heap, surrounded by liquid poop, unable to even get up to clean herself. She kept slipping and sliding back down. The clean-up was massive. They should have paid the custodians extra that week. But fortunately or unfortunately, depending on how you looked at it, Gorilla Girl survived. And in two weeks she was back at school, albeit a few pounds lighter.

But because everyone thought she would wreak havoc on every kid in her special education classroom, they put her temporarily in a different homeroom—mine. *AND* changed her locker to be right next to mine. I was beyond angry, but there was nothing I could do. For the first time in my life, I prayed that my mother would move to a new school district. No longer able to escape and with not a sound coming from my firefly, I relied on my survival instincts to guide me.

For the first week, I was careful not to get in her way. I'd wait until she had gone to her locker, then I would open mine. One day I waited and waited, but she never came. I thought that perhaps she would be absent, but my guess was wrong. As I bent down to open my locker, I felt a hot breath on the back of my neck. As I turned around, I was greeted with a creature from my most disturbing nightmares.

Gorilla Girl grabbed me by my blouse and pulled me near enough to her face that I could see a close-up of her thick red lips and tiny, baby-sized teeth. Her hot breath smelled like sour milk. Teen acne spread over her forehead and cheeks. And there was a thick, scary-looking rash covering her neck and forehead.

"You poison me," she snarled, her eyes radiating pools of blackness.

"I-I don't know what—"

"You poison me! Dey told on you. Dey saw you wit dat bottle. You poison me."

Before I could say another word in my defense, she tightened her grip and threw me against the lockers so hard that I temporarily blacked out, either out of fear or loss of breath. Then before I knew what was going on, I began to fight like one possessed. Everything was moving in a merry-go-round blur. I couldn't see anything, but I could hear kids shouting, "Fight, fight, fight!" I knew I was being hit, but I didn't feel anything. I did feel some pressure, but no pain.

I grabbed her short greasy hair, but my fingers slipped through unable to gain a grip. My skinny arms were moving rapidly as I kept pounding hard on her big, scary torso. I kept ripping at her shirt, desperate to grab hold of something to gain leverage. I kicked and scratched and punched. And just like that, it was over. Two teachers and a hall monitor pulled us apart. I finally realized I had been sitting on top of Gorilla Girl, straddling her massive body, but I wouldn't let go. I'd gone too far to the edge of sanity and it would take some coaxing to bring me back.

"Sandy, Sandy! Let her go! Let her go!" yelled one teacher. I struggled to understand her commands.

As they pulled me up, I still held onto her shirt, ripping it off and exposing her dingy underwear. Blood was covering my torn, open shirt. I wasn't sure whose it was, since I had yet to feel any pain. I staggered to my feet.

"Get washed up, both of you! And put your shirts back on!" yelled the vice principal.

Looking down, I saw that my buttons had been torn off my blouse, exposing my bra-less chest. I quickly closed it, as if I had something to hide. I was as flat as a Swedish pancake. My hands were covered with blood.

There were so many kids and adults around that I never got a good look at Gorilla Girl. They took us to the principal's office separately. But first, I was ushered by the hall monitor to the girls' bathroom, amid the cheers of the kids who'd come out of their classrooms to watch the fight.

When I got inside the bathroom, I looked in the mirror and barely recognized myself. My hair—what was left of it—was sticking up in every direction. One eye was droopy and swollen. My bottom lip was fat, and blood was oozing from the cut inside my mouth. I looked like the loser in a heavyweight title fight. *"—And in this corner, Sandy Forte weighing in at—"*

But at least I was alive. I had fought the great gorilla and lived. I had no idea of the damage, if any, I inflicted upon her and I didn't care. I was just happy to be breathing.

Gorilla Girl and I were suspended for two weeks and my mother had to come up to the school before I was allowed back. I was upset, not because of the suspension, but because I'd have nothing to eat but oatmeal in the morning and beans at night. I really missed my school lunches, but living in Chicago had taught me to take whatever was thrown at me. There wasn't time to reflect on who did what and why. If you did, you might end up in a long line with desperate believers just waiting for something good to happen. It didn't mean I wasn't optimistic. It just meant I'd stopped believing in fairytales.

My wounds had nearly healed. I also found out I had a broken little finger and my hand had deep gorilla bite marks. But Glory had patched me up with alcohol and a torn sheet. Mama was angry that she had to go to the school. She was going to have a baby soon and didn't like leaving the house.

When I returned to school after the suspension, I didn't really know what to expect. As I took my seat in homeroom, Gorilla Girl came in and sat in the front row. She turned and stared back at me. All the kids sat in hushed silence, probably wondering if there was going to be a rematch. Looking straight ahead, I pretended to pay attention to the substitute teacher's commands, which nobody understood or listened to. Gorilla Girl got up from her seat and casually made her way back to where I was. I braced myself for another fight. She looked like she was holding a weapon in her huge left paw. As she got closer, I took out my little hoop earrings I'd stolen from Mama's dresser. *Was I about to die?* She stood over me and placed three new yellow pencils on my desk. As she opened her hand, I could see where she had bitten her nails off to the nubs.

"My name is Amanda. And dis here is for you," she said. She put her hand out for me to shake it. I thought I was having some kind of out-of-body experience. Unsure of what I should do next, I put down the earrings I was clutching and simply shook her hand.

"Bet nobody mess wit her. She my friend," she said as she turned to the class. She gave me an awkward smile and returned to her seat.

Now that my soul had returned back into my body, I tried to figure out what had just happened and why. It seemed that Gorilla—I mean Amanda—was mentally and socially challenged in some way and no one had bothered to get to know her or even tried to help her. —Not the teachers, not the school counselors, not the principal, not even her own family. Because everyone was afraid of her, they simply tried to ignore her or get out of her way.

I had thought of her as worthless, not even deserving to live. I had also tried to kill her off in my own clumsy way. She couldn't express herself. She had to speak slowly, digesting every word. And sometimes she was aggressive. I wonder if all the times when she had taken food, that maybe she had just wanted to connect with the other kids. It seemed it wasn't the food she really needed, it was friendship.

I had stood up to her and we had both been suspended, and to Amanda that meant that we must be alike because we had shared something—we had something in common. Anyway, that was how I saw it.

I looked down at my three yellow pencils, wondering what it had taken Amanda to get them. What she had thought of when she purchased them. My firefly wings fluttered again, creating that tingling feeling that started in the pit of my stomach. But this time as my eyes began to well up with tears, I allowed them to flow, wiping them away with the sleeve of my jacket. And for some strange reason, I wanted to go up to where she was sitting and put my arms around her, but I resisted the temptation. Instead, I put the pencils in my satchel, opened my book, and tried to concentrate on the lesson for today.

FROM GOD TO AMANDA

You're a masterpiece, a divine creation by me
Such a Masterpiece and everyone will see
it's only your temple that's made to hold
such a perfect spirit, mind and soul
And in my image you were made
The product of the price I paid
Not too big, not too small
Not too short, not too tall
I can see my infinitesimal Grace
is portrayed in your wonderful face
the Lord of Host made you who you are
a rare piece of art and my celestial star!

CHAPTER 12

THE SUMMER OF '65

The sounds of summer had arrived in Chicago, and we were finally out of school. Kids were yelling, playing kickball in the streets while music blasted from slow, passing cars. The ice cream man drove his truck to the tune of nursery rhymes, as the big man with the straw hat pulled his cart filled with fresh melons down the street crying, "Watermelons! Fresh waaaa-ter melons! Mel-la-mel-la-melons!"

I wondered if I still needed my firefly light to give me courage. Maybe he thought I was old enough to take care of myself. After all, the firefly had been silent when I fought Amanda a few months ago. But there was one exception. I'd taken the middle school Scholastic Achievement tests and they'd decided I'd skip a grade. I knew why I'd done so well on the test. It was because every chance we got, Glory and I would be in the library reading books. We went there to do our homework because our lights were usually turned off for not paying the bill. And that was where the exception came in. Whenever we went to the library, my firefly seemed to come alive with a fierceness, guiding me to all types of interesting topics like history, science, and poetry. His wings landed on books by authors like Gwendolyn Brooks, Zora Neale Hurston, and Langston Hughes. He glowed when I discovered Shakespeare's sonnets, *Jane Eyre* and *A Tale of Two Cities*. I devoured as many as time would allow. As I sat resting on soft leather cushions, I felt a sense of quiet serenity My mind became a temple filled with imagination and awakenings, bright and warm—the total opposite of our house. We'd stay until we were kicked out at closing time by the ever watchful librarians.

One afternoon, I sat on the stoop of our building while Amanda braided my hair. Yes, I said Amanda. After the near-fatal poisoning on my part and big beat-down on her part, we found that we actually liked many of the same things. She had a great talent for braiding, which Glory and I thought was extraordinary. Her strong, nimble fingers could plait the tiniest of braids in fancy rows.

"Amanda, girl, people should start paying you for braiding their hair," I said.

"What? Naw, I ain't gonna charge nobody no money."

"But you're really good. People would pay a lot of money."

"Nope."

"Why not?"

"Folks who ain't got no money shouldn't have to pay to look nice . . . But—I wouldn't turn down a hamburger and some fries." *There were still some things that we needed to work on.*

The next week when our new sister was born, everybody wanted to name her.

"How 'bout Lucky Lucy. She look lak she gonna bring us some good luck," Charlie Cole said.

"Well, we sho' need that," Mama said as she gave the baby a warm bath.

"Nooo! That's crazy. What about Elizabeth after the queen of England?" I said.

"You think we is royalty? That's a White person's name. I'm thinkin' she should be named after me, *Janetta Mae,*" Mama said as she dried her off.

"Nooo!" everybody said in unison.

"How 'bout Deidra?" my little sister Mary suggested.

"Deidra . . . hmmm. Maybe Dee Dee. That sounds good, don't it Janetta Mae?" said Charlie. A loud chatter erupted in the room. Finally, everyone agreed that Dee Dee would be her name.

One thing about Charlie Cole was that when he got lucky, he got really lucky. That night, in spite of my mama's protest, he went out and got into a game of high-stakes poker on North Avenue. This was a part of Chicago where only the high-rollers went to gamble. So, how this penny-ante hustler got into the game was anybody's guess. He told us he was born with a *gift of gab,* meaning that he could talk his way into anything. So after staying out all night, he came home driving up in a brand new 1965 convertible Bonneville Cadillac. It was neon yellow with white leather interior. As Glory and I watched him get out, I looked down the street to see if he had been followed by the police. Mama was looking out the window and quickly ran down with Dee Dee in her arms. Charlie Cole leaned back on the car with a big grin on his face, looking like a cat who'd just swallowed a canary.

"Well . . . What y'all think?" he said.

"Man, whose car is this?" Mama said.

"Who you think? It's ours, thanks to lucky Dee Dee. I told you she was gonna bring me luck! See here, I gots the title and everything!" He pulled out a thick wad of papers from his pocket and handed it to Mama.

A crowd of onlookers were quickly forming around the car. Glory and I decided to get in the back seat followed by Mary and Lola. Bubba jumped into the front seat and immediately started honking the horn.

"Hey! Don't be messin' around wit nothin'. And make sure y'all' feet ain't dirty," yelled Charlie.

Now that all the neighborhood kids were starting to investigate the door handles and shiny statue on the hood, Charlie Cole had had enough. He got in the front seat with Mama and the baby. Then we all took off down the street like the getaway car leaving a bank robbery.

"Hey, kids. Y'all wanna go for a hamburger ride to White Castle?"asked Charlie, his face beaming as bright as a new penny.

"Yaaay!" we all yelled.

"Now don't go spendin' all our money on no foolishness. And slow down," Mama warned.

"Hey, don't worry 'bout no money. I done won enough to live on for a long while." He pulled out a thick roll of cash from his pocket. As he made a sharp turn around the corner, Mama quickly snatched the money and put it in her purse.

"Hey, Janetta Mae, why don't we go to see yo' mama in Texas? I think we all might be needing a vacation 'round 'bout now."

Mama looked at him with slanted eyes.

"Yeah," she said. "I guess we can stay wit her for a while. Then we don't have to pay for no hotel or nothin'." But before we left, Mama insisted that Charlie trade in the Cadillac for a more sensible, used station wagon.

So that's how our summer vacation started. There was no plan, or plot, or reason. We just headed out. We hadn't even packed a change of clothes, we just went. But I guess it didn't matter how we went as long as we arrived. I couldn't wait to share all my stories with Grandma and finally be home again.

Since Grandma didn't have a phone, there was no way to warn her of what was about to descend upon her. When we arrived in Hooks, we all piled out of the station wagon to the look of shock on her face. There we were—six kids and two unstable adults—coming to spend the summer in her little three-room cottage. But what could she do? We were, for lack of a better word, *family*. So we were welcomed with open arms. Where and how we would all manage to eat and sleep, was something I left to the grown-ups to figure out. I was home again, and that's all that mattered.

The next day, I awakened to an indescribable feeling of my body being burned and smothered by heat. I'd forgotten what it felt like in Texas in July. It wasn't even six a.m. and it had to be well over a hundred degrees in the shade. Nothing was moving outside. Even the chickens had taken for cover in their coop.

What were my *"parents"* thinking? Everyone was laid out on small cots, couches, and oversized chairs, sleeping two by two. Mama and the baby slept with Grandma. I'd slept with Glory, and Lola slept with Mary on a cot. Bubba and Charlie Cole were squeezed together on the tiny couch. Now that I'd gotten taller, Grandma's house looked much smaller than I recalled. Even the ceilings looked lower. If I stretched out my arm, I could even touch it. I felt sorry for my grandmother. It seemed that no one had taken a thought for her—we just invaded. But if she minded, she never showed it. She was busy in the hen house, collecting eggs for breakfast. As I reached the coop, I could hear her singing as she often did when she worked.

"Jordan River—one mo' river to cross—ohh, Jordan River—one mo' river to cross. There be one mo' river to cross, ohhh—"

"Grandma, you need some help?"

"Well, I speck if you gotta mind to, you kin tote some water from the well in that bucket over yonder," she said. She pointed to a large, wooden bucket hanging on the outside of the smokehouse. "And mind you don't spill any. Water's precious as gold in some countries."

Since I last saw her, her face hadn't aged, except for a few minor wrinkles here and there. I wondered what it would be like if she wasn't here to come home to. I grabbed her around the waist. "I love you so much, Grandma!" I said, near tears.

She put down her basket of eggs. "Now what's wrong? Is you all right?"

"Yes, ma'am, I'm all right. I jus' . . . I jus' don't want somethin' to happen to you."

She smiled. "My land! Ain't nothin' gonna happen to me that ain't in God's plan. You ain't gotta be fearin' the unknown. Um gonna be 'round a long time, you'll see. Now go on and tote dat water in the house. Yo' folks be wantin' something cold when dey gits up."

I thought back to that night when the misty fog had covered her face and the words she'd said that I couldn't understand or remember. *What had really happened that night?*

"Grandma, remember when you prayed for me and the misty fog came in and—"

"I pray for all my children every day. I can't rightly recall a mist or a fog."

"It was when I was real little and—"

"We talk about this some other time. Now go on and scoot!"

Why was she avoiding this subject? Does she think I'm still too young to understand?

After supper that evening, the heat hadn't let up and I figured I needed to find an air conditioner fast—somewhere, anywhere. Grandma could see I was anxious so she got a cloth dipped in cool water to put on the back of my neck.

124

"I's fixin' to take a walk down to Cali Mae's house. You wanna come wit me?" she said.

Cali Mae lived next to Peggy Lomax, a quarter of a mile down the road. Her husband, Silas, had gotten some money for getting his hand cut off in an accident at work and they had built themselves a brand new brick house—with air conditioning in every room. After she told me this, it didn't take me long to agree. Glory had retreated into her own world of books, while Mama and Charlie Cole lay sleeping in Grandma's bed with baby Dee Dee. They were still pretty tired after the long drive. Oblivious of the heat, Mary, Bubba, and Lola continued to play in the sand in the front yard.

We walked slow and leisurely down the quiet road, fanning away gnats and mosquitoes. A few cars passed and the passengers waved while straining their necks to see who I was. Since the town was so small and the Black population even smaller, everyone had to be accounted for.

"Grandma, do you like livin' here in Hooks?"

"Well, never lived no place else, so I ain't got nothin' to compare it to."

"I hate my neighborhood, I hate my school, I hate everything about Chicago. I wish we could just stay here, build a house, and live next door to you."

"Well now, you never know what the Lord's got planned—jus' gotta' trust Him."

"So, you jus' 'trust Him'—and you never complain about nothin'? Ain't there somethin' about your life you don't like? Something that if you could change it, you would?"

"Truth is, I don't like lots of things I sees. But I cain't spend my time worrying and complaining. Gots too many other things to do."

"Like what?" I said, quite surprised that she actually had a life of purpose other than being my grandmother.

"Well, let's see here . . . I's got loads of canning to do, now that the fall near 'bout here. And by and by, there's my quilting. I done started five mo' patterns. Gotta have 'em ready fo' winter come. Church be waitin' to give 'em to po' folks. And I's started sellin' my silk cushions I done made. Got five orders already. Not to mention Miss Toad livin' way up there in dem woods, old and blind. I's got to make sure she got her provisions. And I done started Bible study once a week, plus, um a gonna sell this here Tuppaware. And lemme see here . . ."

"Wow, Grandma! I cain't believe you got so much going on."

"Well . . . I tries to keep myself busy." Grandma slowed her pace and came closer to me, as if she was about to say something really important. "Glory done wrote me a letter 'bout how much she wanna come back here to live."

"Glory? She never told me. I mean, she never acted like anything was wrong."

"Naw. She don't share her feelings much, you know that. But still water runs deep, jus' like your mama."

"Deep?" I laughed scornfully. "Mama ain't deep, she's mean and evil. And why is she so selfish? Why she—"

"Stop it. Judge not, lest you be judged the same."

"What?"

"You know, you kin find fault in anybody if you go looking for it. Your mama been through a lot wit these gossipy people 'round here. When she left for Chicago to go to nursing school, she got wit child by some no account and no marriage or ring to show for it. Then she got with child a second time and broke up with yo' daddy."

"Mama said it was on account of he didn't buy her some *big* diamond ring. What kinda love is that?"

"It's true she was selfish. But like I done said before, natural human love is selfish. It only wants what *it* wants. Now it was hard for her to show her face 'round here. And when she did, these so- called Christian folks laughed her out of town. And them Baptist preachers—heck, they didn't waste any time givin' her the left foot of fellowship. And the names they called her . . . well, ain't worth repeatin'. She took care of y'all the best she could—takin' low-payin' jobs and such. She couldn't afford to go back to that nursing school. But she wouldn't give y'all up, no suh. And she wouldn't give up on herself neither. It gave her backbone like a steel crowbar, instead of a cotton string."

I stopped, sinking under the volume of Grandma's words. My mother wanted to become a nurse? I never thought she had any ambitions at all. The distance between us began to shrink. I remembered my first grade teacher asked me what I wanted to be when I grew up and I said I wanted to be just like my mother—nothing. How wrong I was! Now I wanted to know more, but before I could formulate a good enough response, we found ourselves on the front lawn of Miss Cali Mae's house.

CHAPTER 13

REDEMPTION

Everywhere I land
on shore or on the sand
I light up!

breaking curses that remain
generations of invisible chains
I light up!

I Am the Lamb exposed
the crushing of a single rose
I open doors that fears have closed
I light up!

and in His face
redemption lies
an angel soars across the skies
I light up!

I bring new songs of hope to Earth
a gift from One who gave new birth
I light up!

The house was small but well-built with an immaculate rose garden landscaping the walkway path. As we walked up to the porch, the door had already swung open.

"How do, Miss Minnie Bell!" Cali Mae said warmly. She had a pattern of freckles across her broad face, and a welcoming, wide smile accentuated by one gold tooth in front. As she ushered us in, I felt the rush of cool, soothing air. It startled me as it blew down from the vents above our heads.

"Hope you don't mind us stoppin' by to visit for a spell," said Grandma.

"You know you is always welcome," Cali Mae said as she pointed to the couch. "And who is dis here child? Dis yo' grandbaby?"

"Yessum, she sho' is. They all just came in from Chicago last night."

"Don't say? The whole family?"

"Yessum, that's right."

"You must be Janetta Mae's daughter. Look just lak her by the eyes," Cali Mae said as she stared at me.

"Yes, ma'am. I'm her daughter all right."

"How long y'all plannin' on stayin'?"

"I don't know, ma'am," I said. I wasn't paying much attention to her questions. I was just exhilarating in the delightful invention of air conditioning.

As we sat down in her small living room, I took notice of all her furniture. It looked as if no one had ever sat on it before. Her sofa, love seat, and two armchairs were white tufted silk and completely covered by a thick clear plastic. Even the baby-blue carpet had a sheet of plastic covering it. The entire decor was done in a French Provincial style that I'd seen in one of the magazines at the library. There were ornate coffee and side tables with tops made of white marble with painted gold rims. The white-and-blue lampshades were dripping in gold fringe. Huge tapestries of dancing angels in heavenly places hung on the walls right next to pictures of the Trinity: Jesus kneeling on a rock, President Kennedy and Martin Luther King, Jr. There were so many porcelain cherubs on walls, tables, and shelves that I began to count them. I wondered how she managed to get so much stuff into such a small space.

Cali Mae brought out teacakes and iced sweet tea in tall glasses, which I quickly gulped down.

"So how long you planning on stayin'?" she asked me for the second time.

"I believe she done mentioned dat date ain't rightly set as yet," Grandma said.

"Did I already ask her that? Well, bless your heart! My memory is gotten so poorly lately, I even done bought me some medicine for improvement, but my land, I forgits to take it," she said, smiling.

Then we heard another visitor coming up to the porch. It was Peggy Lomax.

"Well, come on in heah, Peggy," Cali Mae yelled. "I got company and I ain't fixin' to git up to open that door."

I noticed she had grown much taller and lankier. She wore a white headband and some sort of black synthetic-looking hairpiece that hung down to her waist. She had on a tight, white mini skirt with a red-and-black-checkered shirt tied in the front. It was all pulled together with white high-heeled sandals and an oversized white purse. It seemed she was trying much too hard at looking older. She had to be at least thirteen years old now, and she had the pimples to prove it. Her aim at sophistication had missed the mark by at least a mile, which made her not nearly as pretty as she used to be. *It seems the good Lord gave her ashes for beauty.*

"How doin', Miss Minnie Bell? How doin', Miss Cali Mae?" she asked.

"Yo' school friend Sandy done come back here from Chicago. Show yo'self friendly and say hi," Cali Mae said, sipping her sweet tea.

"How do, Sandy?" she said, still standing in the doorway.

"Hi," I said. I couldn't see her face very well, but from where I sat, she looked scary.

"Peggy Lomax! You knows better din to keep my door open in dis here heat. Why don't you gals go on in the kitchen and git some cold soda pop?" Cali Mae suggested. Peggy quickly closed the door as I stood up.

The kitchen was a bit simpler, but no less perfect, right down to the canisters in the shape of teddy bears with angel wings. But I counted only about eight or nine golden angels on the walls. I think it was because the space was limited by her fancy Sears catalog, electric stove and refrigerator.

"So, how long you stayin?" Peggy asked as she flipped her fake hair around her shoulders.

"I dunno." I looked away so as not to appear too interested and opened the cola bottle.

She was wearing some strange kind of perfume. It smelled like a mixture of lilacs and turpentine. And upon closer inspection, I noticed she had on a face full of makeup. It began with the thick application of black mascara, matting her top eyelashes together, followed by a ghastly ring of black eye pencil below.

"You know, I gots my period now," Peggy said with pride.

"Well, I guess you better watch out wearin' white short skirts."

"Not right *now,* stupid. *And* I wear a *B* cup bra so— Anyway, my brother, John Lee, says all his buddies think I'm really cute. You know he turned 16 last week. And you know Punkin, Leroy's brother? Well . . . he paid me one whole dollar just so's he could feel 'em. Iffin they gits any bigger, um gonna start charging a buck fifty."

I just looked at her. I couldn't believe that I had envied her all these years. I had actually wanted to be her. Her life was what my fantasies were made of. She had a mother and father who loved and took care of her, and a big brother who protected her from bullies. She had a big house in Hooks, with a pink bedroom and a white canopy bed. She had everything—except she didn't know it. *What was her problem?*

"*And* I kin drive now," she continued.

"Right. Next thing you be tellin' me is you're a millionaire with an airplane parked in the driveway."

"You ain't that important for me to be lyin' to, if that's what you think."

"I'm not thinking nothin'. But I do know somethin'. I know you ain't old enough to get no driver's license."

"I didn't *say* I got a license. I said I could drive. And you don't need no license in Hooks County to drive if you got a written permit. You don't know nothing 'bout the laws round here."

"Whatever you say," I said. It was true. I didn't know much about the local laws, but I did know you needed a valid license to drive a car anywhere in the USA.

"I'm fixin' to take my brother's car and go for a ride. You wanna come wit me?"

Okay. I had been gullible enough to fall for her tricks before, but not this time. And besides, I knew she didn't like me, so why would she want to spend time with me?

"Your brother ain't gonna let you drive his car. And even if he did, —no thanks."

"Okay, suit yo'self. But I knows dis here boy who used to be sweet on you last time you was here and I bet he's still sweet on you. But I ain't gonna tell you who he is 'cause you too chicken shit to come out and meet him . . ."

"Meet him?"

"That's where I'm goin', silly. I'm gonna go over his house in

132

Texarkana and play records. You know, have a little fun. I heard he done bought a brand new Hi-Fi system, and I thought you might wanna come along to see it. Ain't nothin' else to do around here, or haven't you noticed? But if you thinks um just lyin', then I goes by myself," She took another sip of cola.

I thought about how I had misjudged Amanda before I really got to know her. Perhaps Peggy Lomax just needed someone to go that extra mile for her. As she continued to talk, I felt a coldness, like a hard piece of white ice had begun to form right in the pit of my stomach.

"Well . . . uhh . . . how long you planning on stayin'?"

"As long as you want. Um only goin' on account of you."

It would be interesting to see a boy who already liked me. I remember when I went to the only colored school in Hooks County across the road from Aunt Hattie's house. I was in grade 4B and there was this boy named Marvin Lee that I had a secret crush on. He was much shorter than me, but he had curly, brown hair and nice eyes. I caught him looking at me several times and I remembered him being the smartest boy in the class. He could recite his multiplication tables all the way to the twelves. And he always had a gold star on the bulletin board for math. I wondered what he might look like now. As I thought on those things, that piece of ice slowly melted, like a snowball in hot Texas sunshine. It was replaced with a feeling of excitement that seeped through my body like lighter fluid, igniting a sense of adventure in me.

"Well?" she said.

"Listen," I whispered, "we have to be back in an hour, *one hour*, or my grandmother is gonna have Charlie Cole out lookin' for me. You understand?"

Grabbing my hand with a desperate sense of urgency, she pulled me up from the table. "Let's go!"

We snuck out the back, running to her house next door. Breathlessly,

I waited outside as she swiped her older brother's car keys while he sat with a bottle of root beer watching wrestling on TV.

The car was a very old, beat-up green Pontiac whose best days were far behind it. Rusted and dented in on both sides, the door to the passenger side could barely open. The back window was broken out and the windshield cracked. It took her several tries before it actually started. The exhaust fumes were so powerful, I began to choke.

"Don't worry, you'll git used to it," she said.

As we sped along the highway going at least seventy-five miles per hour in a forty-miles-per-hour zone, I cringed at the thought of us running out of gas on the highway.

"Why don't you turn on the lights now? It's dark outside," I said.

"Lights don't work," she giggled. "And we is just about out of gas, so we better git to his house fast."

I couldn't believe what I'd just heard, but I didn't have time to process it because we had now pulled into a gas station.

"Fill 'er up!" she said to the attendant. "By the way, you got any money?"

"Why would you even think I have some money? Do it look like I got a job?"

She laughed. "Well, it looks like we gotta pull the ol' *okedoke*!"

"The what?"

When the gas station attendant finished filling up the car, he came over to the window.

"That'll be—"

Peggy took off, speeding out of the station, doing a U-turn in the middle of the street until we were back on the main highway.

"Now that be da okedoke!" she yelled with a mad gleam of excitement on her face.

I closed my eyes. I was sure that a police car was closing in on us somewhere and we'd be hauled into jail. Then she did what I thought was the impossible. She careened off the highway, tires screeching, veering down a barely lit side street in Texarkana. I sat there, my heart beat like a native drum, —getting louder and louder. I didn't know if we would hit someone or if someone would hit us. With no lights, I didn't know if we would crash into a tree or a house or a person. I didn't know if I would die that night or ever see my family again, or if I would ever tell my mother that I had judged and misjudged her without hearing all the evidence. I silently prayed that my firefly hadn't left me because of my foolish pride. I did need him. I needed him more than ever. Then Peggy stopped the car.

"I wanna git out—now!" I screamed as I pulled at the broken door handle.

"Listen, Miss Chicken Shit. You ain't goin' nowhere. You is staying wit me till we gits back home. Now, I cain't find dis ol' boy's house, 'cause it's too dark and I done forgot where he live. I stopped on account of I think we gots a flat tire."

She got out, checked the tire, and got back in. "Naw, it's still holdin' up," she said. She took out a stick of gum from her white purse and began to chew, popping it loudly.

I knew I couldn't escape the car even if the door handle actually worked. Where would I go in a strange city? How would I get back home? She turned the car back on. It sputtered a little, but started right back up, and with that we were off, speeding back down the pitch-black road to hell. She ran over a large pothole and we both bumped our heads on the roof of the car, but finally, through some divine act of fate, we reached a main street. With my eyes being closed most of the trip, I felt safe enough to open them again. As I looked out at the streetlamps, a huge sense of relief washed over me, like rainfall down a windshield.

"Ain't dis fun?" she asked, with a wink.

If she hadn't been driving, I seriously thought I would've strangled her to death. Out of the corner of my eye, I could see the front of her shirt had opened, exposing a wad of white tissue paper peeking out of her over-stuffed bra. *Lies, all lies.* When Uncle Zippy said everybody had a firefly inside them, I'm sure he'd never met Peggy Lomax. She was as empty as the fake bra she was wearing.

Finally, she seemed to have developed an extra molecule of sanity and common sense. She found the highway route that lead us back to Hooks County. As we drove along the highway, she turned the volume up on the radio and sang along with *The Supremes*. I was glad she was using her horrible voice singing rather than talking to me.

Suddenly, from nowhere there appeared a large truck seemingly coming straight towards us. I hadn't even noticed that when she'd taken her eyes off the road to change channels, she'd veered across the lane into oncoming traffic. I braced myself for the inevitable impact. Oblivious to our impending death, Peggy was still singing loudly, admiring herself in the rearview mirror. The trucks' horn sounded a fierce warning, but it was lost on her, as *"Stop in the Name of Love"* blasted from the radio.

As the truck loomed closer, its bright lights became blinding, flooding the inside of the car. All this had only taken seconds, as time seemed to evaporate, leaving me only enough to scream out a warning— but no sound came out of my mouth. I was frozen. I looked over at Peggy Lomax, realizing she would be the last thing I saw on Earth. I closed my eyes and imagined the face of my grandmother crying. All of a sudden, I felt the strangest sensation of floating. I opened my eyes slightly to see what was happening. It was as if I was being carried high up in the air on a rollercoaster and being turned upside down then right-side up. The car lifted off the highway, landing smoothly into a ditch.

As I sat there, I became aware that Peggy was gone. She had been thrown down to the floor of the car. Then a bright glow caught my eye from the cracked front windshield. There he was. He was more than ten feet tall and wore some sort of glowing white uniform. I had to shield my eyes as I tried to figure out if this was real or some strange dream. His skin was bronze, and his hair was a long, black braid down his back. And when he saw me look at him, he smiled. As he turned to leave, that was when I saw them. They were magnificent. Two large wings protruded from his shoulders. They were see-through with the appearance of brilliant, multicolored stained glass. I watched as he ascended upward until there was only blackness.

That's when I found my voice. I screamed and Peggy Lomax, who'd been knocked cold, woke up.

Illustration by Marlon Hall

"Wh-what's goin on?" she asked.

"Didn't you see him? Didn't you see his wings?"

"Wings? What in Sam Hill is you talkin' 'bout? All I know is we gotta get this car back befo' dat ol' boy find out it's gone," she grunted as she got up from the floor of the car. "And why you grab hold of the steering wheel like that?"

"What?" I asked, confused. "I didn't. I mean, I don't remember. I never—"

"Well, it don't make no never mind. C'mon, we gotta go!"

I was still too stunned to move, but I managed to understand that we had to get back home.

I forced myself to crawl out of the car. We had landed in a small ditch off the highway. Upon examination the car hadn't been damaged too bad, and I felt okay. But Peggy Lomax had a large bump on her forehead. We both pushed with all our strength, but the car wouldn't move. So she went up to the road and flagged down a family, who were driving back to Hooks. They all got out and helped push the car, until it was back to the curb. The father even put on the spare tire. I was glad they were new in town and didn't know who we were. By some miracle the car started and we were off again.

"Now don't you go runnin' yo' mouth off to yo' grandma about what happened tonight," she warned. "We's in enough trouble as it is."

"I won't say anything, I promise," I said.

We drove in silence the rest of the way. When we reached her house, she turned off the engine, coasting as she turned in, and parked the car as far away in back of her house as she dared. I could see the lights were on at her house. She got out, came over to my side, and opened the door.

"All right, git! And you bets not tell nobody, or—"

Just then, the back screen door opened, and footsteps came towards the car.

"You bets keep yo' mouth shut!" she warned again as I took off into the darkness for Cali Mae's house.

The door swung wide open. It was Cali Mae. Her face beaded in sweat, even with the air conditioner on full blast inside.

"Miss Minnie Bell done already went home lookin' fo' you. You best be gittin' along," she said, closing the door.

As I turned to leave, I heard a commotion and looked towards Peggy Lomax's house, I could just barely make out two figures in the moonlight. Peggy had been caught by her big brother, John Lee, as she'd tried to sneak into the backwoods.

"What the blazes I done tole you 'bout stealin' my car? Ain't I done warned you?" he yelled.

I saw him open his hand as though he was reaching back into Africa, and slapped her hard across the face. As she fell to the ground, her wig came flying off from the force and landed beside her. He bent down trying to pull her back up, but she cowered deeper towards the ground.

At first I wondered if I should try to help. *Maybe I should ring the doorbell and alert Miss Cali Mae.* No, this was one battle Peggy would have to fight on her own. I turned to run, then I stopped abruptly without knowing why. That's when a warm sensation came over me. Suddenly, I was transported to when I'd felt helpless and alone on Johnson's Creek, hoping someone would come to my rescue. And Leroy had appeared like God's little miracle. So would it be justice if I abandoned her when God hadn't abandoned me? And even now, God had sent an angel to protect us both from sure death.

I raced over to where John Lee stood empowered with a new sense of bravery. Peggy Lomax was still lying in a heap on the ground.

"Leave her alone! I told her to take your car," I lied.

"And who the Sam Hill is you?" he asked, in astonishment.

"I-I-I'm her friend."

"She ain't got no friends." He started moving menacingly towards me, and I backed away.

"Leave her alone, John Lee!" Peggy yelled. She got up on her elbows and fell back down again. I could see she had a big bruise over one eye and thin trickle of blood ran from her nose, glistening in the moonlight.

"And if you messes wit me, my daddy from Chicago gonna come lookin' for you and whip you good," I said lying again. He came closer, his hands balled into fists. "I . . . I hear him comin' down the road right now. Yep, that's him walkin' . . . carrying his rifle. You hear that?" I turned towards the road pretending to look for Charlie Cole's ghost. John Lee stopped and tried to listen. That's when I took my chance. I turned and ran without stopping until I reached my grandmother's house. She was standing on the porch with Mama and Charlie Cole. Grandma spotted me first, as I ran into the yard shaking.

"My land! Why you try to scare us all to death lak dis?" Grandma said. Her voice reached inside me making me draw back.

"Mama, I told you dat girl was all right," my mother said, holding Dee Dee on her hip. "She ain't got a bit of sense. She like to run away like dis all the time. I don't pay her no never mind."

Taking a long stretch, Charlie Cole got up from the porch steps and headed for the car. "Well, I'm fixin' to go for a ride. Janetta Mae, you want to come along?"

"Might as well." She followed him to the car.

I ran after her, grabbing her around the waist. "I'm sorry, Mama— I'm sorry for . . . —for—everything."

"Girl, what you talkin' 'bout? Go on in the house."

But I held onto her, burrowing my face into her chest. This time she didn't pull away. Holding on to her meant holding on to the hope that someday we would find the right words to say I love you and mean it.

Slowly she began to stroke my hair. "It's all right, it's all right now," she said, in her deep, low whispering voice.

As I lay in bed that night, I relived the moment again and again of what it felt like being held by my mother. I'm sure she held me when I was a baby, but this was different. It was like piercing through a looking glass and embracing life itself. This helped me put the ordeal with Peggy Lomax far away from my conscious memory. Just having survived it was a real miracle. What I had witnessed tonight couldn't have been a dream. It was reassurance that my firefly hadn't left after all but had been transformed. He was no longer a tiny invisible creature or even a cherub like the ones on Miss Cali Mae's walls, but he was a giant, strong enough to pick up a car and move it to safety. And his job was to watch over me, making sure I got back home to safety. I knew I could never tell anyone about what happened. For one, they wouldn't believe me. Two, Grandma would never trust me again, and three, I promised Peggy Lomax that I'd never tell. And even though it had all been her fault, I could only hope that her brother had mercy upon her.

The next morning, it had gotten a few degrees cooler and there was even a slight breeze moving through the maple tree in the front yard. Leroy, whom I barely recognized, brought over a bushel barrel of peaches and put them on our front porch. All the kids grabbed and devoured them like furious savages before Grandma could wash them first.

"Hi, Sandy," Leroy said shyly.

"Hi, Leroy. Killed any rattlesnakes lately?"

He smiled, revealing a row of perfectly white teeth. He wasn't at all chubby anymore. He had grown lean and tan with even a few muscles poking from his arms. I would even call him good looking for his age, although I still didn't know exactly what that was.

"Nope. I ain't killed nothin' but time. Me and Bo' Dean fixin' to go down to Hinman's farm and pull up stumps. Kin I stop by later on this evening? Maybe we kin catch up. That is, if it's all right with your mama."

"I'm sure she don't mind," I said.

"How 'bout you, Miss Minnie Bell?" he asked.

"Well now, Sandy too young to be courtin' boys. But I speck it's okay if you come before eight and see here dat you leave by nine-thirty. That's my bedtime."

He smiled again shyly, then jumped off the porch and disappeared back into the woods. *Well, don't that beat all?* Leroy was sweet on me despite all the teasing I had made him endure. Maybe he had liked me all this time and I'd never noticed, or had I even cared? And then, wonders of wonders, Peggy Lomax rode by full speed on her bicycle, her long wig flowing in the wind. She gave a quick wave and kept going. I couldn't see her face, but from all other appearances she seemed to have survived intact from her brother's attack.

Later that day, I sat next to Grandma as she sat rocking on the front porch. I realized she was the only person I felt comfortable enough to share my feelings with. For as long as I could remember, she had always listened to me without judgment or reproof.

"Grandma, ain't you the least bit curious what happened to me last night?"

"Well, I speck if you want me to know anything, you'll git around to tellin' me."

I hesitated. "Uh . . . have you ever seen a real angel?"

"No, cain't say I have. Have you?"

"Um . . . well . . . it could have been a dream, or maybe—"

"Well, we all got our own personal angels made by the Lord to watch over us. But you never gits to see 'em wit your naked eye 'cause he's a spirit . . . Unless, of course, you in real danger of dying befor' yo' time, then he shows himself, wings and all."

"Oh," I said solemnly. I knew that this would certainly be the end of our conversation about angels and I'd better just change the subject. "I don't want to say it, but I got sucked into Peggy's scheme of going into town last night. She said we was just gonna go on a joy ride and that we was comin' right back!"

Grandma never looked up. She kept right on rocking. "Sounds like what dem White slave masters told the Africans before they put 'em all on the ship." She winked at me, but I was serious.

"Well, I still think I hate her. And I'll never trust her again."

"What you say? Hating somebody's the same thing as murder. I better not ever hear you say you hate anybody! You hear me?" She stopped rocking and stared at me, eyes blazing. I could see I'd stepped over the gospel line.

"I guess I don't really hate her, but she sure makes it hard for somebody to like her. But I kinda understand her a little more than I did before. So . . . I'm sorry for saying I hate her."

Her composure returned and she started rocking again. "Don't tell me, tell God."

"But Grandma . . . she's an awful liar."

"And you ain't never lied? I ain't making no excuses for who she is or what she done, but everybody's entitled to forgiveness, even Miss Peggy Lomax."

I guess Grandma was right about that, but I couldn't ever imagine myself forgetting what she had put me through. I wondered how my grandmother could have lived a life so rich with forgiveness and so empty of malice.

"Grandma, how can I learn to be perfect? I really want to be, but—"

"Hush up! Cain't nobody *learn* to be perfect."

"So how come you always seem to say and do exactly the right things?"

She laughed and laughed, as though I'd told the biggest and best joke in the world.

"Truth is, I cain't count how many times I've missed it. Maybe hundreds of times. But you learn from what you do wrong, not from what you do right. Besides, you already is made perfect when you was born. You just like a new, little green apple on a tree. At first, it might be hard and bitter— ain't fit for nothin' much—sure enough cain't make no pie wit that kind of apple. But the Lord done said it's just perfect in the stage of development it was in. Then it starts gettin' bigger and takes on some red color, —starts to get ripe and juicy. Lord knows it's perfect in that stage too. You just gotta know what stage you in and don't stay in it too long or you just go rotten and fall to the ground. Only thing you is good fo' then is fertilizer."

As I listened, I realized there would be a lot of things in my life that I would get wrong, giving me plenty of opportunities to learn. But I'd want to get some things right the first time too. I'd just have to recognize what stage of development I was in. And maybe . . . just maybe, I could get to the point of forgetting and forgiving Peggy Lomax. But I didn't think I'd reached that stage just yet.

Grandma went inside to rest, but I stayed awake a little longer just to think and sort things out. Mary came out and sat on my lap.

"Will you rock me?" she asked, as she looked at me with big brown eyes.

"Sure."

As I rocked her back and forth, I wondered why everything was the way it was. But who knows why things are what they are. They just are. Even my firefly. What would have happened if I hadn't swallowed it? Maybe that didn't have anything to do with it. Maybe he was there all along. I used to wonder if my firefly would ever leave. Now, I believe he was a gift—not from my Grandma, but from God Himself. And once you get a gift from Him, it couldn't ever be taken back. I looked at Mary.

"You know something? I still got heaps of faith and fire that I ain't even used up yet."

"Used up?" she asked.

"Un huh. And so do you. You see little sister, it doesn't matter how small and insignificant you are, you can still transform the universe. Because there's a gift put inside of everybody, when they're born . . . even you. You just have to learn how to use it—like your hands. See?" I took both her hands in mine. "You were born with hands to reach down into the dirt and pull up as much hope and happiness as you can carry—you might pick up a pebble and throw a stone. Just be careful where you aim. And don't let your blaze go out. You don't want to shrink down in the shadows like a plant searching for the sun."

"No, I don't wanna do dat," she said, as she drifted off to sleep.

Just then I heard a faint whistling sound approaching us. As the full moon lit up the gravel road, I could just make out a tall boy walking towards the house. He was wearing a gleaming, white tee shirt and a smile as wide as heaven. The firefly began to stir.

EPILOGUE:

Although the past may have roughed up my wings a little, they're still able to fly me towards my destiny. That's because I'm perfect in my stage of development, just like Grandma said. As a matter of fact, I think in my next stage I'll become a glowing, iridescent butterfly. Or if I believe hard enough, I could even become a fiery, purple dragon. And by the time I'm done, the only thing left will be ashes of mishaps and misfortunes. And why not? The only hindrance to faith is not believing in yourself. That's why I'm never gonna give in to doubt, because I don't want to rob the Earth of what God has called me to be.

Illustration by Marlon Hall

GLOSSARY

Here are some words used frequently in this book that you should know. They are words that come from southern dialect and Black culture. Definitions are also included.

betcha	I bet you
cain't	cannot
chunking	throwing
dar	there
dat	that
din	then
dis	this
dunno	don't know
fo	for
gimme, gimmie	give me
git, gitten	get, gotten
haints	ghost
heah	here
heathen	A person who is not a Christian
iffin	if perhaps
inquisition	When someone is being questioned repeatedly
jus	just
lak	like
lessin	unless
Philistines	Bible group who were against the chosen of God
poor unfortunates	Those who have no hope for their future
reprobate	A person who is unable to become a Christian
sho	sure
sto	store
unarm	To catch a person off their guard or by surprise
unrepentants	Those who have not asked to be forgiven by God
wit	with
y'all	you all *Often spoken in place of a name to one or more persons*
yessum	yes ma'am

About the Author

Sandra Brown Lindstedt graduated from Lewis and Clark College, where she received a Bachelor's Degree in Theatre. She lived in New York working on and off Broadway. She has written and directed numerous plays in USA and in Sweden where she now lives with her husband Christer. This is her first children's book.

About the Illustrator

Suzanne Groat is a self-taught artist from Portland, Oregon. She currently resides in Kansas City, Kansas. Although she is a nurse by trade, she has always had an appreciation for different types of art and vibrant colors. For the last several years, she has been painting primarily as a hobby, using acrylic on canvas. Her paintings include landscapes, trees, wildlife and a series of dancing girls. Life of a Firefly is her first adventure as a children's book illustrator.

Made in United States
North Haven, CT
14 July 2022

21374213R00087